I0578936

LOST

in

TIME

TRAPPED IN A PREHISTORIC WORLD

DAN ARTHUR BUSBY

1

C H A P T E R

Jimmy stood directly in front of a judge, in a situation playing out his own personal nightmare. Accused of murdering a co-worker, he had been thrust into a grueling trial. The whole thing had been so unbelievable, that he pinched himself to be sure it wasn't a dream. The fact that he knew he was innocent made matters even worse, as the prosecutor brought up seemingly overwhelming evidence against *him.*

Now the painful ordeal was over, except for the sentencing. The jury had just issued a guilty verdict, and the judge scowled at him from his lofty perch. Shaking his head in contempt, he spoke to Jimmy. "It's my responsibility to get filth like you off the streets, and that is what I will do. You are hereby sentenced to permanent banishment to the cretaceous period. May God help *you.*"

Jimmy's knees trembled and grew weak. Officers on both sides of him had to lend support, as he *fell.*

The year was 2040, and the judicial system had found it very economical to dispose of hard core criminals in this way. The perfection of the time machine was harnessed and controlled by the state. Not paying for lifer criminals was the way to balance the budget. No one, however, could have or use a time machine on their own ac*cord.*

Jimmy felt himself being dragged away. He finally got his legs back, and kept pace with the officers, who then hustled him out of the building, and into a police car. His destination turned out to be a holding cell at the police sta*tion.*

A frame with a thin cot was the only piece of furniture he had. He sat on the cot, hands folded and elbows resting on k*nees.*

Jimmy stared at the floor, and slowly shook his head in unbelief. He knew all about the cretaceous period. It was the most active period in history for dinosaurs. Explorers had been sent there, and most of them barely escaped with their lives. Some did not escape from the huge carnivores that roamed the *land.*

Jimmy, at the age of 25, had been active in time machine technology. He had always been at the top of his class, and earned two degrees in the field. Ironically, his chosen career would now facilitate his ***doom.***

Condemned criminals, if given a choice, would to the man or woman, choose life imprisonment over banishment to the cretaceous period. The idea of being eaten just didn't set well with most f*olks.*

"Jimmy." He suddenly snapped out of the trance, and looked up. The jailer was standing outside the bars with a sympathetic look on his face. "For what it's worth, I think you're innocent." He started to turn around, but hesitated. "They'll be transporting you in the mor***ning."***

Jimmy nodded. "Thanks." He forced a s***mile.***

2

CHAPTER

The next day Jimmy was taken across town to a large building that housed the time machine. Security was tight, as he was escorted via elevator to the basement. Stepping into a small room, he and the two officers approached what appeared to be the door of a bank vault. A man was waiting for them, and began working a combination lock on the **door.**

With a loud clank, the door opened slowly, exposing a dark room. The three men moved into the room, and the lights switched on. Then Jimmy saw it…the invention that he had worked so hard on, along with a group of scient**ists.**

He knew exactly how it worked. The man who opened the first door then opened this one. It looked like a submarine door. He turned a wheel to open a tightly sealed entrance. The man spoke to the guards. "You can release **him.**"

Jimmy felt their tight grasp disappear, and he staggered briefly in front of the open door. Inside he could see the small chamber of the time machine…with only enough room for maybe three people to stand clo**sely.**

The door man looked at Jimmy sternly, but held up a hand as if to stop him. "Before you step in, I have something for you. They didn't say I couldn't give it to you, and I'd like you to have it." Opening a large cupboard, he pulled out the likes of an elephant gun, along with a backpack. "It is loaded. It takes six rounds at a time. In the bag are one thousand rounds." He nodded and pursed his lips, then summed it up quickly. "Good **luck.**"

The man didn't have to order Jimmy to walk into the chamber. He knew it was time, and took three steps, stopping squarely in the center of the cha*mber*.

Suddenly the door slammed, as though his fate were permanently sealed. He held the gun and backpack tightly, took a deep breath…saying goodbye to the only world he had ever k*nown*.

3

CHAPTER

He thought while standing there, about when they were doing tests on time travel to the cretaceous period. Several times the men were transported directly into dangerous locations. A few were attacked and killed by large be*asts.*

For years the government had been sending prisoners with no way of tracking them. Who knows how many of them survived the initial journey, or whether any of them were still a*live?*

His thoughts were interrupted by a humming sound, indicating the mechanism was in action. He tightly gripped his weapon, knowing the landing may not be *soft.*

Suddenly he felt a strong wind at his back, followed by the collapse of the floor. Jimmy seemed to fall a couple of feet, landing firmly on solid rock. He was no longer in the chamber. A bright sun beat down upon him, and the temperature was at least 20 degrees wa*rmer.*

Quickly, he assessed his surroundings. He was standing on a slab of rock, but all around was thick jungle and tall trees. Making sure the safety was released, he positioned his weapon while scampering off the *rock.*

It was difficult to decide which way to go, and he hesitated, not wanting to make a foolish deci*sion.*

A voice then burst through the air. "Hey! Over here!" Jimmy squinted to the right, following the sound. His eye caught a man waving his arms, and standing at the base of a *tree.*

"Quick! It's safe over here!" Jimmy lost no time. He sprinted through waist high ferns to the large tree, where the man was already ducking into a cave. Having no desire to linger, Jimmy hastily foll*owed.*

Inside was an area of about ten feet square. The man he had followed sat down on a rock, motioning for Jimmy to follow suit. He sat on another rock, noting the man's appearance. He seemed fairly young, but had a long beard. His whole demeanor was scruffy, calloused, and d*irty.*

"My name's Rick." He held out his hand, and Jimmy gripped it gladly. Rick continued. "Man, it's good to see another human. At least a live *one.*"

"Jimmy forced a chuckle. "I know about the danger here. I helped to create the time machine. I'm J*immy.*"

Rick seemed surprised. "Huh, I just assumed you were a prisoner like me." "Oh, I'm a prisoner. I didn't commit the murder, and I got railroaded." "Wow." Rick nodded. "That sounds very familiar. Same here." Jimmy's curiosity was aroused. "How long have you been *here?*"

"A little over a year now." He pointed to a series of marks on the wall. Then he eyed the gun in Jimmy's hands. "That is a powerful looking weapon. Did they give that to *you?*"

Jimmy nodded. "You mean they didn't give you anyt*hing?*"

Rick shrugged. "I've been using wooden spears. For food, I've gone mostly to pl*ants.*"

Jimmy glanced at the light streaming through the cave entrance. "Have you had any close calls with preda*tors?*"

Rick broke into laughter, which stopped just as quickly, as it started. "Almost every day I have a brush with death." He nervously jabbed his spear into the sandy cave f*loor.*

"I've seen dozens of men appear from the time portal, but have never laid eyes on them again. I finally decided to try and stop them as soon as they arrived. I thought we could band together to give us a better chance of surv*ival.*"

Jimmy squeezed his gun barrel. "Well, I can tell you that I'm glad to run into you. I think forming a group is the only way to survive long *term.*"

$$4$$

CHAPTER

"I was lucky to find this cave." Rick spoke while slapping the rock he sat upon. "But there are creatures that roam during the night. I have to sleep next to the opening to ward them off. Sometimes I can get a fire started, which keeps them *away.*"

Jimmy shook his head. "I can't imagine what you've been going through. With my help, your quality of life should imp*rove.*"

"I'm delighted to have you." Rick smiled. "But right now we should gather food. In the heat of the day the predators are resting in the shade. In the evening they come out. That's when we stay in the *cave.*"

"Lead on then." Jimmy offered. "I'll be right behind *you.*"

Rick grabbed a handmade basket and slithered outside. Jimmy followed, clinging to his gun, and wearing the ammo back*pack.*

Rick knew exactly where he was going. He slowly slid along, with his back flat against the rock wall. He gripped his spear with two hands, and peered around the corner. He then signaled to Jimmy to move forward with him. The two men jogged a short distance through fern, stopping at a large berry p*atch.*

"Ok," he began working at once. "Help me fill up this basket as fast as poss*ible.*"

Jimmy started picking immediately. The berries were blue, and about the size of his fingernails. They looked like nothing he'd ever seen before, but he did not take time for ea*ting.*

The only noises were from birds in the trees. Within five minutes, the basket was full, and Rick signaled to begin the return *trip.*

Halfway back, Jimmy was horrified by a monstrous, gut-wrenching roar. He felt as though a huge beast was right behind him ready to clean up. He started to freak out, but Rick turned around waving both arms and shaking his head. "It's okay." He spoke in a loud whisper. "Let*'s go!"*

Sprinting ahead to the cave, he ducked down and scrambled through the opening. Jimmy frantically swung around, waving his gun in every direction. The ground shook with each massive footstep. As he fell to his knees at the cave entrance, he looked and saw a big head peeking around the corner. This beast knew where he was, and was giving chase. He threw his rifle into the cave, and scooted in at maximum s*peed.*

No sooner had his feet cleared the opening, than an explosion occurred just outside. The dinosaur was very upset at missing a meal, and commenced stomping the ground, and slamming against the rock. The cave was thick and impenetrable, but Jimmy retreated to the wall, shivering as he pointed his gun at the entr*ance.*

5

CHAPTER

When the dinosaur finally stopped attacking the entrance, and disappeared, the two men sat in silence. The only noise was heavy breathing from both of **them.**

Rick sighed. "That one came from nowhere. I guess that's the close call for the **day."**

Jimmy shook his head. "Well, that was way too close for me. There's got to be a safer way than this to sur**vive."**

A hearty laugh came from Rick's direction. "I'm open to suggestions. I've been doing this for a year, and it's getting more and more dangerous around **here."**

Jimmy was puzzled. "How far have you travelled from **here?"**

Rick, who sat with his back against the wall, chuckled. "When I first arrived, I was inexperienced, and wandered about a mile south of here. They all must have been asleep that day. Doesn't often happen, but I ended up down by the river, and saw something interesting. It looked like a small entrance to a cave, but when I crawled in, the place was huge. May have been the size of a h**ouse."**

He paused for a moment. "I headed back to tell Simpson about it. Well, he was killed before we ever made it **back."**

Jimmy thought for a moment. "Wow. You know that sounds a lot more promising than this. I say we go back there and try to improve our quality of **life."**

Rick inhaled slowly, then exhaled. "They only reason I would even consider it, is your gun. And I don't know if it would even slow down some of these dino*saurs.*"

"I know I'm a new comer," Jimmy reacted, "but it seems to me that we would have more room and a closer water supply. My question is, what's the best time to tr*avel?*"

"The same answer as before." Rick sounded confident. "In the heat of the day. There are occasional exceptions to the rule, but by and large, they are resting when it's ***hot.***"

"Okay." Jimmy could see Rick's silhouette in the dark. "So would that be about ***now?***"

Rick replied in earnest. "We've got to give the T-Rex, or whatever that was, time to wander off. I'm not going anywhere right ***now.***"

The duo ate their berries while resting, recuperating from the trauma they had just experienced. After a short nap, they ventured out again… slowly. Rick carried the ammo and led the way, while Jimmy followed closely with his ***gun.***

6

CHAPTER

The men looked around constantly while they travelled slowly. At the corner of the rock wall, they turned right. Suddenly a thud was heard, not far behind them. This sound was followed by grunts and gr*oans.*

Looking back, they saw the form of a man rolling around in the fern. He quickly stood, and they could see he was carrying a gun like the one Jimmy *had.*

Rick hurriedly ran closer, calling out. "Hey! Over *here!"*

The man saw him, and immediately ran toward him, while Jimmy kept a watchful eye for danger. As Rick led the man forward, the three met in a ci*rcle.*

"Okay," Rick began. "My name is Rick, and this is Jimmy. What's your *name?"*

"I'm Glen." The man volunte*ered.*

"Good." Rick continued. "We don't have time to talk. Just keep with us, and be ready to use that we*apon."*

Glen nodded, while he checked his *gun.*

"Let's go." Rick moved forward quickly, keeping away from an animal trail. He edged forward through waist high fern, followed by Jimmy, and Glen bringing up the *rear.*

All was quiet except the sound of fern brushing against their bodies. Nerves were on edge, but Rick, having lived here for a year, had a feel for the environment. He kept close to the tree *line.*

Their journey continued without interruption for 15 minutes. They hung low in the fern, and took refuge in the trees. Then a change of landscape developed. A rocky ridge grew and veered left, with a thin line of trees at its *base.*

The three men found themselves walking beside a few trees and a sheer cliff on one side, with a river just a few feet away on the other side. Still Rick seemed to know where he was going. He confidently led the way, but slowed down just before a bend in the river. He turned around and flashed the stop sign to Jimmy and *Glen.*

His suspicions were justified, as the sound of a huge branch breaking ripped through the air. The men jumped behind the trees and crouched down, hiding as best they could. A low growl caused their very bones to vibrate. Their hands shook, as Jimmy and Glen checked and rechecked their *guns.*

More growling combined with heavy footsteps followed. The men could feel the earth move with each *step.*

No one dared speak, but they could hear the great beast approaching, and knew they may have to open fire on this huge pred*ator.*

The footsteps grew closer, and then they had a visual. Moving along the river bank was a towering dinosaur, walking on its hind legs. Its head wagged from side to side, as though searching for something that it sensed was t*here.*

Glen and Jimmy quaked in their boots, and nervously squeezed their triggers. Then the beast seemed to catch their scent. It stopped, looking directly at them. It froze for a moment, then reared back its head. The roar that followed was so loud, that the men felt entirely exposed. Jimmy and Glen both dropped their rifles from pure fright. However, they both had the wherewithal to pick them up a*gain.*

Suddenly the creature lunged forward to their position. They had time only to raise their weapons and fire six rounds apiece, until both were out of ammo. The giant beast fell against the trees, and staggered backward, keeping its balance, and making a high pitched roaring sound. It thrashed its head and neck from one side to the other, stomping into the river. With one great bellow, it tipped forward and splashed into the w*ater.*

Jimmy and Glen were petrified, still kneeling like statues, with their guns raised. Rick pulled them back to reality. "Hey, guys! Reload your wea*pons!"*

7

C H A P T E R

The two jumped at the suggestion, grabbing ammo from their backpacks. Within seconds they were loaded, hands shaking uncontroll*ably.*

Rick leaned toward them and whispered. "It's not much far*ther.* Follow me and keep q*uiet."*

The two gunmen stood up and tried to follow Rick, but their legs felt like spaghetti. Their pace was slow, but steady. They continued to travel next to the trees, which were a few feet from the r*iver.*

Rick could now see a distance up river, and knew his destination was not far away. He kept an eye on the rock wall to the left. The trees would disappear, and there would be a small opening in the *wall.*

Jimmy and Glen watched carefully for any sign of wildlife. They were still in shock, and felt as though they were dreaming, yet were keenly desperate to find she*lter.*

Rick led the way for another five minutes before spotting his destination. "This is it!" He looked over his shoulder, and shuffled up a small sand bank, stopping in front of a cave. Its measurements looked to be roughly two feet tall by one foot *wide.*

As the other two men caught up to him, he explained. "I've been in here before. It's not too dark to see. Just follo*w me."*

Rick got on his hands and knees, slowly peering in to see if the cave was occupied. Scooting all the way in, he quickly turned around. "Come in, let'*s go!"*

As Glen crawled through, Jimmy checked around one more time. His eye spotted three mid-sized carnivores who were running down river, apparently toward him. While he watched, they picked up speed, going for the chase-*down.*

Wasting no time, he ducked in and scampered through. Within five seconds, they hit the rock wall, roaring and clamoring a*bout.*

The men stood inside the cave, watching the legs of the beasts until they left, tussling and squabb*ling.*

Jimmy shook his head. "You really take your life into your hands out t*here.*"

"It's what everyone needs to learn." Rick added. "Or you won't last *long.*"

He turned and examined the interior of the cave. As they all gazed, they noticed a flat rock floor with walls that rose to ten feet. On one side of the cave was a vaulted ceiling. At the edge of the ceiling were small holes where day light shone thr*ough.*

Jimmy noticed some large rocks that could serve as chairs. He took off his backpack, laying it down with the rifle. "Looks like we're safe for the moment. We should *rest.*"

The others agreed, and followed suit. Jimmy breathed easy for a minute, shifting his gaze to Glen. "Sorry your arrival was so harsh. Mine wasn't much better. I landed about an hour before *you.*"

Glen forced a grin, still shaken up by the near death event. "It's tough to instantly switch from the 21st century to a time like *this.*"

Jimmy folded his hands for a brief moment. "I'm glad we connected when we did. Survival is doubtful if you are alone. Rick and I decided we need to stick together, and work as a *team.*"

"Oh, I'm all in on the teamwork part." Glen sounded enthusiastic. "Just let me know how I can *help.*"

Rick joined in. "The most important thing right now is finding a way to protect ourselves. I suggest we stay here and work things *out.*"

He focused on Glen, whose image was dark, but seeable. "So Glen, do you have any skills that might help us in the way of surv*ival?*"

"Average survival skills." Glen spoke, then inhaled deeply. "But I know how to make iron. And from all the yellow and red rock around here, we could have a big opera*tion.*"

Jimmy perked up. "This could really save our lives! With iron, we could make weapons, build fences, and many other th*ings.*"

"That's right." Glen nodded. "I need a fire pit to melt the ore into a bloom, and pound it into whatever shape we **need.**"

Rick pointed at Glen. "You should focus on iron. That definitely opens up great possibilities for us. My job will be gathering food, mo*stly.*"

Looking at Jimmy, he queried. "Jimmy, what do you have to o*ffer?*"

"Smiling, Jimmy began. "My main goal is to eventually open up a time channel to get us out of here. But in the meantime, I could assist both of *you.*"

Rick laughed heartily. "Gentlemen, we have a plan! Let's get **busy!**"

8

Chapter

The men first went out together in search of food. It didn't take long to find nut and fruit trees, including something that was similar to coc*onut.*

After feasting, they went back out after pitch that was plentiful in the trees. They also brought in wooden stakes for application of pitch to make torches. In the same operation, they collected massive leaves from short plants, which would make comfortable bed*ding.*

Rick carried flint rock, and was able to light up a torch for better visibility. The first thing he saw was a man-sized hole at the far end of the *cave.*

One by one they crawled through, and stood together on the other side. They listened quietly for a moment. "Wow". Rick said as he raised the torch higher. "I can't see far, but this sounds like a huge cave". Every noise echoed off the w*alls.*

As Rick inched forward, the rock floor trended down*hill.*

Jimmy and Glen followed single file. The grade was a gradual decline, and after a couple of minutes, began to level *off.*

Now they could hear water dripping. Rick turned the torch to the left, revealing a large pool of water, with seepage off the w*alls.*

"This is a spring!" Glen sounded amazed as he s*poke.*

"Let's see what's to the right." Rick commented as he swung the torch and continued the walk. A rock wall loomed to the left, and another began on the right, forming a narrow passage way. They followed along for another minute, veering to the r*ight.*

The narrow trek suddenly opened up into a vast space. The floor reflected bright ye*llow.*

Glen squatted down and examined the rock. Most was iron ore, but not all. He picked up a yellow rock the size of a golf ball. "I don't believe it." He gasped. "This is pure gold." Checking around, he found gold scattered all over, but iron ore was in much larger quantities. "This iron is what I need to transport up front. When I get a big enough pile, I can mel*t it.*"

Searching around, Rick found the room to be a dead end. He smiled. "Looks like we have the basics of what we need." He led the way back to the front *cave.*

The men first rolled one of the big rocks in front of the opening for safety from roaming creatures. They then lay out the big leaves as bedding for the night. Feeling secure, they relaxed on their beds before falling as*leep.*

"Glen," Jimmy spoke, "I'm curious about where you acquired iron making sk*ills.*"

"Worked in steel production." Glen answered without hesitation. "I can make just about anything from steel." He raised his chin. "But what I'd like to know from you is just how will you get us back to the 21st cen*tury?*"

Jimmy nodded and half smiled. "Fair enough. That's my area of expertise. It's made possible by the magic of a newly discovered agent called Ben*zole.*"

He rose up on his elbows. "When coconut bark is burned, the Benzole in it has an effect on time. When the smoke is allowed into the higher pipes, it moves into the future. When pushed through the lower pipes, it travels into the *past.*"

"Whoa! Hold on a minute!" Glen was flabbergasted. "Are you saying we can make a time machine using coconut *bark?*"

Jimmy chuckled. "Well, yes. That's the main active element. Of course, we'll need bamboo pipe to channel the smoke. I'm also thinking of constructing a steam powered flying platform to keep us out of harm's *way.*"

Rick laughed. "I'm trying to figure out if you're for real or not. Some of that sounds pretty fanta*stic.*"

Jimmy didn't hesitate with an answer. "Oh, I know what I'm doing. I've made time machines and flying machines before. How do you think we got *here?*"

"Okay," Rick conceded, "but in the wild with no modern material or t*ools?*"

"It's just a matter of understanding chemistry and physics." Jimmy explained. "If we had iron, the whole thing would be feas*ible.*"

9

C H A P T E R

Over the next two weeks the men planned together and worked hard. Glen actually fashioned a few metal objects, including a big hammer for easier metal shaping. Jimmy and Rick gathered fruit, nuts, coconut, and gr*eens.*

None of the men stayed out in the open any longer than necessary, and then not without a gun. Their purpose was to be as self-sufficient as possible, and at the end of two weeks, things were lookin*g up.*

One afternoon it was supper time inside the cave entrance. The men sat on three large rocks…two torches providing l*ight.*

On the menu were nuts and fruit. As Glen gathered a handful of nuts, his brow wrinkled. "This may sound crazy, but we really need to get out of this *cave."*

Rick and Jimmy showed blank looks, but momentarily Rick responded. "I can't wait to hear how we could build a dinosaur-proof house. I mean, it would be great to get out of here, but are you ser*ious?"*

"Absolutely." Glen was emphatic. "Only we don't have to build a dinosaur-proof house…just the perim*eter."*

Jimmy nodded and smiled, as though something had just occurred to him. "There's a large flat area on the bluff above us. Your structure would have to be super strong, but that is the ideal spot, overlooking the *river."*

Glen agreed. "Not only will the wall be super strong, but we are going to have devastating weapons on each *side."*

Eyebrows raised as Glen spoke. He continued. "I will make huge metal springs, which will be able to fire long, sharp metal poles. These guns will be mounted on swivels for maximum accuracy. I'd say if we had two on each wall, we should be well *armed."*

Rick shook his head in disbelief. "I had no idea your iron making could have such far-reaching results. If you can do this, go for it! We'll all work toge*ther."*

"Like I said," Glen returned, "I can do anything with iron. This is going to take a while, but it will get us out of this cave, and we can stop living like gophers. We can build a house within the wall bounda*ries."*

"Are you sure the iron spears will have enough power to impale those big dinosaurs?" Rick que*ried.*

"That is what I'm most confident of." Glen confirmed. "The poles will only be two inches thick at the bases, and the tips will be razor sharp. The force in these springs will be devasta*ting."*

Jimmy thrust an arm into the air. "Why delay? Let's start at *once!"*

10

Chapter

The next morning they began anew with a strong determination to succeed. Their work consisted of two main chores. The first was iron production, and the second gathering *food.*

Glen and Jimmy helped Rick harvest enough food for the day, then they all pitched in with the *iron.*

Glen found a naturally concaved area of rock that served nicely as a smelting pot. This was conveniently located directly beneath the vaulted ceiling that had cracks to the outside, which would allow the smoke to escape. He had fashioned a big metal table for pounding the iron into s*hape.*

The work was tedious because each man carried a hammer, chisel, and basket for carrying chunks of ore from the mining room. A bucket was used to store loose pieces of gold, which were found lying around. The gold would be useful in building different th*ings.*

Glen developed an organized approach to his work. He knew which item must be built before the next, and before long was constructing the main supports of the wall. These were solid square bars that measured 6 inches thick and 20 feet long. His plan was to have a bar every four feet. Each side of the wall was to be 60 feet long, so 240 feet of wall were needed. This meant about 60 bars were required. Smaller cross bars would sit horizontal to the main *posts.*

Jimmy and Rick were a little skeptical about how long the project would take. But soon Glen proved them wrong. Within two months, all

60 of the main posts were done, and that included fittings for interlocking p*arts.*

In another two months, the cross bars were done. The men had stock piled all of the wall parts on the plateau above the cave, and were beginning the assembly pro*cess.*

They had to be vigilant at all times to maintain safety. A few close calls happened with huge flying dinosaurs swooping down to grab one of the men. These large pterosaurs were silent, and gave no warning of their appr*oach.*

It was decided that one man should be on guard duty while the other two wo*rked.*

Jimmy was the guard today as Glen and Rick struggled to lock pieces together so that one corner would stand up on its own. They finally persuaded a corner and two side bars to interlock with the cross *bars.*

Glen gazed up at the erect structure. Placing hands on hips, he smiled. "That's the beginning of the fortress." He excla*imed.*

At that moment a large tree branch was snapped in half. As the men looked up, a carnivore, bigger than Rick had ever seen, stood 30 yards *away.*

Jimmy reached down and picked up the extra gun, tossing it over to Glen. Glen quickly snatched it up and slowly back peddled toward the trail that led down the face of the cliff. All three men moved in the same direc*tion.*

Rick went down first, having no weapon. He backed down the steep trail, using hand holds to steady him*self.*

Jimmy and Glen faced the giant, nervously pointing their guns. Glen spoke softly. "Go ahead. I'll follow you *down."*

Jimmy began climbing down, still with a finger on the trigger. The huge meat eater lurched forward, rapidly closing the gap. Jimmy saw that they weren't going to get down the trail in time, so he pointed his weapon with one hand. Glen stood at the brink of the cliff like a statue, pointing his *gun.*

The monster gave a mighty roar as it moved in for the kill. "Fire!" Glen hollered, and immediately both men began emptying their guns. The beast did not slow down, and tried to nab Glen with one big snap of its jaw. Glen avoided the onslaught, but fell backward and off the c*liff.*

Jimmy still hung on the edge with his right hand, and clutched the gun with his left hand. He had discharged four rounds, and had two *left.*

The dinosaur towered over him, lifting its head high in the air for an ear-splitting roar. It then glared down at Jimmy, who had crawled down another step. The great jaws opened, and swung down toward Jimmy. Hugging the rock with his body, Jimmy raised the gun with his left hand. As the open mouth approached him, he fired the last two rounds directly into the oral ca*vity.*

The last thing he remembered was sliding out of control down the face of the c*liff.*

11

CHAPTER

Jimmy awoke lying on his bed inside the cave. He lifted his head and blinked, recognizing Rick and Glen sitting on rocks. He suddenly felt a sizable pain in his head. Raising an arm, he felt a large bump on the back of his head. "Wow." He exclaimed in disbelief. "What happ*ened?*"

"Well it's good to see you're among the living." He detected a note of gratitude in Rick's voice. "We really weren't sure if you were going to wak*e up.*"

Jimmy rose up on his elbows. "Oh, that hurts. It's coming back t*o me.* Must have hit my head when I *fell.*"

"I do think you guys wounded that dinosaur." Glen sounded confident. "It ran away pretty *fast.*"

Jimmy rubbed his head again, gazing at Glen. "It's bad news if we didn't kill it. Don't know how you made it, Glen, the way you *fell.*"

Laughter came from the rocks. "Fortunately, Rick softened the *blow.*"

"Well, it wasn't so soft for me." Rick interjected. "But neither of us was hurt too bad, and we were able to drag you back to the *cave.*"

Jimmy slowly sat up, feeling stiff and sore. Rising to his feet, he shuffled to the vacant rock and had a *seat.*

Glen's face reflected the flicker of a nearby torch. His short red beard shown in the light. "We're going to have to get back up there and continue to *work.*"

Silence followed these words, as though a sentence of doom was just pronou*nced.*

Rick bowed his head and nodded reluctantly. "I know that's true, but we really must have a better escape *plan.*"

Jimmy rubbed his face in thought. "I believe I know the solution to our problem. The cliff is roughly 20 feet down. We should construct a soft landing, so we can simply jump off when we're threat*ened.*

Rick raised an eyebrow. "Exactly! Probably a six foot pile of palm leaves would do it. It has to be broad enough for all three of us to jump at the same *time.*"

Glen heaved a sigh. "Sounds logical to me. It's a decent way of escape, but we still must keep a closer watch for approaching da*nger.*"

"Agreed." Jimmy acknowledged. "Let's rest and get started again in the mor*ning.*"

The men tried to recuperate after their narrow escape. They slept extra-long hours, and woke up refre*shed.*

It took only two hours to gather palm leaves along the river, and make a sizable pile at the base of the c*liff.*

After climbing to the top, they scoured the horizon. "What is that?" Jimmy pointed to a spot no more than 30 yards *away.*

Then it became apparent what it was. "You certainly did kill it." Rick barred the way with his arms as he spoke. Small, but ferocious looking scavengers came into view. They saw the men and snarled fiercely. They then went back to feeding on the carcass, keeping one eye on the intru*ders.*

"Back away." Rick uttered softly, as he started to retreat. Jimmy and Glen readied their weapons, as the men stood at the cliff, waiting for any developments. They slowly started their routine, with one of them on guard *duty.*

12

C H A P T E R

All day long different animals fed off the dead dinosaur. By the end of the day nothing was left but the skel*eton.*

The men were able to assemble one whole side of the wall, which was 60 feet. The big vertical posts were four feet apart, and the smaller horizontal bars were layered at one foot inter*vals.*

Rick was the first to try out the safety jump. His landing was soft and easy. Jimmy and Glen followed suit, grasping onto their guns as they leaped. They were amazed at how nice the landing *was.*

Encouraged by the productive day and the new escape route, the trio vowed to let nothing stop them from finishing the walled perimeter. With renewed energy, they went to work each day and found they had completed the project within a *week.*

The men stood on a rock floor, surrounded by a virtually impenetrable iron *wall.*

"This is just what I envisioned." Glen announced, as he raised a fist into the air and gri*nned.*

Jimmy laughed. "I see it as our first step toward getting our lives back. We'll be able to relax in a comfortable home, and start working on a time mac*hine."*

"Absolutely." Rick joined in the celebration. "But the next project should be to install weapons around each wall. Then I'll feel safe enough to sleep *here."*

Glen dedicated himself to finishing the spring loaded spear guns. He worked long days, with the assistance of the other. The men decided on three spring sites for each of three sides, and two for the ledge *side.*

Working long days, it took a week to construct the spears. Following this was one week for the springs, and a week for the hous*ings.*

Glen hadn't tested the spear shooters, but he seemed to know they would work. Hands on hips, he stood admiring his work. "We are now safe from anything this place has to o*ffer."*

Jimmy turned to Rick. "Have you seen them bigger than the one we shot a few weeks *ago?"*

"Not bigger," Rick ran a hand though his thick hair, "but I've seen them travel in packs, and use team work to *hunt."*

Jimmy smiled. "Well, I hope they don't seek vengeance for lost family mem*bers."*

Glen shook his head. "It doesn't matter. We'll still kill *them."*

"I love your confidence." Rick spoke emphatically. He looked around the wall. "Next up is bamboo 8 feet tall around the entire perim*eter."*

Glen clapped his hands. "The sooner the be*tter!"*

The men soon approached the bamboo fields, each carrying a razor sharp machete. They found their work to be easier than anticipated. With one swing they were able to cut down a large *pole.*

13

C H A P T E R

Within two days they had cut, carried, and stacked enough bamboo. They also had plenty of tough vines to tie down the ba*mboo.*

On the third day they were making great strides putting up the poles. Three sides were done, and they were tackling the fourth and final side when an interruption occu*rred.*

Glen, responding to a noise, looked up and instantly knew he was going to be able to test his handy *work.*

A behemoth carnivore of a different variety came crashing through the trees, stopping at 20 yards. It seemed to be sniffing out fresh meat, and was hell-bent on finding it. Its body was twice as thick as the others they had seen. Its whole appearance was brutish and muscular to the ext*reme.*

The three men were shocked momentarily, but soon recovered, and each sprinted to a loaded spear gun. As if this were not dramatic enough, two more dinosaurs of the same variety came prowling up behind the *first.*

The lead creature opened its mouth and issued an ear-splitting roar, viciously shaking its head, and shuffling from one foot to the o*ther.*

The men clutched their spear guns, swiveling them in attempts to establish good aim. None of them, at this point, was sure the structure would really keep these giants *out.*

The closest dinosaur suddenly leaped forward and slammed against the wall, causing it to shutter. It did, however, remain *firm.*

The defenders desperately rotated their spear guns to point at the monster. It moved quickly, turning around and heading out 20 yards again. It clawed the ground with huge hind feet, and the men were amazed to see what appeared to be smoke shooting out its nostrils. With no warning, the beast shot forward for another violent *crash.*

Glen was ready this time, and just before the big smash, he pulled the trigger. His aim was true, as the spear shot out faster than the eye could see. It lodged nicely in the body of the carnivore, half sticking out its back, and half in the *front.*

The terrible looking animal teetered two feet from the wall and fell to one side, causing a mild earthq*uake.*

Glen didn't waste time, but ran to the pile of spears, and manhandled one into the metal casing. He pulled a lever that reset the spring for another ***shot.***

The other two dinosaurs, observing this development, didn't like the results. They both roared and sprinted at full speed toward the ***wall.***

Jimmy nervously aimed at one and fired. The shot was wide, and the spear just grazed off the side of the creature. This angered the beast even more, and it strutted up to the wall, banging hard into it. The structure, once again, was solid, but by now the other dinosaur was attacking in the same manner. They both slammed their heads and bodies up against the ***wall.***

Jimmy struggled to reload, as the others strained to get a clear shot. Finally one of the assailants moved back, as if to get a running start. This put it into spear range. Rick and Glen took aim and fired simultaneously. Both spears thrust through the beast within a foot of each other. It uttered no sound, but simple stood motionless for a few seconds before falling over like a ***tree.***

The remaining behemoth then seemed to intensify its efforts. It continued to roar and plaster itself against the wall repeat***edly.***

Jimmy finally reloaded his weapon while his friends were going after more spears. He sensed that the attacking monster was too smart to step back as the first two had. It ceaselessly railed against the wall at close *range.*

Jimmy turned his spear gun to the sharpest possible angle. The dinosaur moved in and out of his imaginary crosshairs, so he just held it at that angle, hoping for a shot. After what seemed like several minutes, he suddenly got a good shot. When he pulled the trigger, the spear seemed to explode forward. An instant later, he saw the spear land 30 yards away. To his shock, the dinosaur crumpled to the ground. The spear had gone straight throug*h it.*

14

CHAPTER

Rick and Glen still swiftly reloaded their guns, after which they stood and looked around. All was quiet, as they each stood by their loaded spear *guns.*

The three massive motionless bodies outside the wall almost immediately began to attract atten*tion.*

From the air and over land, creatures of all kinds and sizes started arriving to claim their share of *meat.*

Rick began moving toward the cliff door. "I recommend we go down to the cave until this is cleared out." Jimmy and Glen agreed, and all three vacated the *area.*

The men sat around in the security of the cave, going over what just happ*ened.*

Glen grabbed a handful of nuts and berries from a bowl constructed of bark strips. "I think the structure is solid." He popped some food into his mouth and sat down. "So we are ready to work on the buil*ding."*

Rick snorted and shook his head, showing a sarcastic grin. "The whole time I was ready to forget the spear gun and pick up an elephant gun. I know I was just freaked out. The wall was creaking a lot, but it did hold *well."*

Jimmy agreed. "Sure, this was a petrifying experience. Yes, the wall held nicely, but there's something we need to change about our approach. We can't let them get that close. We should shoot them before they get to the *wall."*

Glen, who still munched on nuts and berries, stuck a finger into the air. "I agree that we should go after them as soon as we see them. But I have an idea that will greatly assist us in that department. We'll fasten metal spikes around the bottom of the wall. They'll angle outward at 45 degrees to stop the approach of large ani*mals.*"

Rick's face lit up. "Of course!" He was ecstatic. "We'll be able to sleep securely, and sa*fely.*"

Glen nodded. "We'll also place metal rods between the top of the wall and the rooftop. That will protect us from air att*acks.*"

The men's excitement over the proposition showed with shouts and high f*ives.*

That night as they slept, they dreamed of a safe haven in the midst of a barbaric and violent w*orld.*

The next day they went up and reclaimed their spent spears. Nothing was left but skeletons outside the wall, and all the bones were cleaned to a shine. Resetting their weapons, they started a routine of labor that went on for three more months. Glen's iron magic continued to work won*ders.*

The day arrived that found their project complete. Vicious looking spikes protruded outward against any would be attacker. A network of rods sealed them in against flying pteros*aurs.*

Their new home was built with plentiful bamboo poles tightened with vines. It was a two story structure with several rooms on each level. The windows were open and breezy to suit the hot cli*mate.*

15

CHAPTER

Jimmy sat at a bamboo table doing notations. He used iron ore powder for ink, which was stuffed into a hollow stick. He scribbled onto large sheets of thin bark. He appeared to be getting excited over his mathematic calcula*tions.*

Rick and Glen lounged on bamboo cots along the wall. Suddenly Rick sat up, showing an inquisitive look. "Make any conclusions yet, J*immy?"*

Jimmy glanced at Rick, quickly returning a gaze to his work. He squirmed in his chair before vigorously nodding his head. "This should work. I'll draw specifications for a lightweight wood stove made from iron." He momentarily eyed Glen, then continued. "We'll have to hook bamboo pipes to this. They have to run in certain precise directions. We'll also need an iron rod so we can attach a large wooden prope*ller."*

Glen continued to lie on his cot, but spoke up. "I'll get that done in two days. Just give me the p*lans."*

Jimmy drummed his fingers on the table, and smiled at Rick. "We're going to build a steam powered helicopter. Then we'll start with the time mac*hine."*

Rick returned a grin as he stretched out again on the cot. "Let me know what I can do to *help."*

As it turned out, Glen was correct. It took two days to complete the iron work. Jimmy stood in awe, staring at the wood burning stove. The metal protrusions stuck out like appendages. At the openings were even screens to filter out the sparks, which could burn the bamboo p*ipes.*

The men stood on a large deck which was built above the house roof. Jimmy's spirits were greatly lifted by the things they had accomplished up to *now.*

Hands on hips, he smiled, affirmatively nodding. "We're only going to concern ourselves with building this steam powered helicopter." He looked from Rick to Glen. "For simplicity, we'll just call it the 'R*iser'.*"

A burst of laughter shot from Glen. "Naming it before it's even built, ar*e we?*"

Rick chuckled. "That's okay; he's just trying to convince himself that he can work mira*cles.*"

Jimmy pursed his lips, moving forward two steps, and turning around. "You guys have no idea. I'm not just shooting in the dark here. I told you I know what I'm d*oing.*"

He grasped the stove and manhandled it onto its side. Picking up two bamboo poles, he eyed both of his coworkers. "I'm telling you ahead of time. Be prepared to be daz*zled.*"

16

CHAPTER

Jimmy did act like he knew what he was doing, so the others just stood back and watched, pitching in to help when they *could.*

Within a few days, the stove was converted into a steam engine. This engine would run on any kind of wood. For time travel, a certain amount of coconut bark would have to be added, but they wouldn't worry about that right *now.*

Glen received instructions on how to make a compression chamber to attach to the stove. This he did in one day. With that completed, Jimmy and Glen worked closely to build a rotor assembly while Rick cut down a hardwood tree to start fashioning a propeller. The men struggled with these jobs for a week before they finally conquered them. They then pieced together a bamboo platform with side r*ails.*

The final very important touch was to place a smaller propeller on the shaft with controls at shoulder level. This could swivel 360 degrees, and its sole purpose was to steer the flying mac*hine.*

At long last the men stood on the roof deck next to the 'Riser', which they had not yet seen rise. The moment of truth had arrived, and a fire was started in the s*tove.*

The blaze was hot, and the pressure intense, when Jimmy finally decided to give it a try. Rick and Glen stood on the deck looking on, while Jimmy opened the stove door and tossed in a couple more pieces of wood. He reached to a valve above the stove and slowly released the pressure. Slightly crouched, he looked up at the main prop. It budged, then rotated slowly. Its speed steadily increased, and suddenly flipped into high *gear.*

A loud humming sound commenced, followed by platform jerking, after which the whole thing began lifting off the deck. Jimmy fell backward, and grabbed onto the side rail. Rick and Glen gazed up from a few feet away, with mouths gaping *open.*

Jimmy felt himself moving straight up…five, ten, twenty feet. He pushed himself off the rail, grabbing the shaft. Gripping the secondary prop lever, he rotated it. The prop burst into action, causing the entire Riser to wobble because the handle was twirling around. Hastily, he grabbed the handle, stopping its incessant 360 degree course. Holding it steady, he quieted the rocking motion of the *craft.*

Taking a deep breath, he peeked over the side rail. Rick and Glen stood in the same spot, but were getting smaller…100 feet and coun*ting.*

This was alarming, going so high on the maiden voyage. Reaching for the pressure valve, he decreased its output, causing the main prop to slow down. The craft seemed to level *off.*

Glancing at the scenery, Jimmy noticed a huge body of water about ¼ mile away. He steered in its direction, having intense curiosity. Against his better judgement, he continued the course. The terrain consisted of thick forest and jungle. Travelling through the foliage were some carnivores. He also saw some huge, long necked herbivores grazing on the *trees.*

Several minutes passed, and the craft was approaching the shoreline. The water was vast, and he wondered if it was salty or fresh. Once out over the water, he was astonished, as he lowered altitude. Literally jumping out of the water were countless large *fish.*

Jimmy shook his head in amazement, but suddenly snapped back to reality. This was only a test flight, and he was out in very dangerous territory. Quickly, he turned the pressure valve back up, gaining altitude. Grabbing some wood from the pile, he flung it into the fire, slamming the *door.*

17

CHAPTER

e began to worry about his situation. Thus far things had gone according to plan. But if anything happened, it could mean lights *out.*

Turning the prop handle around, he headed the Riser in a homeward direction. He kept to a high enough altitude to be safe from land animals. However, he neglected to consider danger from the air. Twenty yards to his right, he saw a large pterosaur, just gliding at his own speed. The creature seemed to have a keen interest in him. He realized he did not bring his gun, so he had no defense. One collision of the beast into the main prop would send the craft down like a rock. If this were to happen, he did not want to have such a high elevation that he couldn't survive the *fall.*

Jimmy lowered his altitude to just above the tree tops. The pterosaur had done likewise, and was closing in on him. If he got ten feet closer, there would be a crash. Jimmy gritted his teeth, bracing for impact. When an explosion seemed inevitable, the flying dinosaur suddenly screeched loudly and disappeared from sight. Jimmy turned around and saw nothing. Instinctively, he peered over the side rail. His eyes trailed downward, where they met a gruesome scene. The pterosaur had been pulled down by a tall agile carnivore, and was now in its meat grinding *jaws.*

His eyes bugging out, Jimmy grabbed the pressure valve and rotated it wide open. Up he and the craft went, all the while continuing to journey toward *home.*

Swallowing hard, he squeezed the prop handle without realizing *it.*

He found it difficult to accept living in such a harsh w*orld.*

He kept alert, searching for the familiar two story house with the deck on top. Several minutes went by before he finally caught sight of it. Soon it became apparent that Rick and Glen still stood on the *deck.*

Jimmy slowly maneuvered his way down to the deck, dropping the bamboo platform softly onto it. Turning the prop valve and pressure chamber valve, he just stood while the noise dissip*ated.*

Rick and Glen stepped forward in anticipation, while Jimmy rubbed an arm across his fore*head.*

"We thought you were a gonner." Rick broke the silence. "Wasn't it supposed to be just a short *test?"*

Jimmy acknowledged with a nod. "Yeah, I'm sorry I got carried away. But…" His tone changed to intense excitement. "I do have some good *news."*

He stepped over the railing and onto the deck. "First, as you know, the Riser runs perfectly. Second, we now have an unlimited source of fish. We just have to figure out how to catc*h it."*

Rick and Glen stared at each other as they followed Jimmy down the ladder to the first floor for some *R&R.*

CHAPTER

The men sat around a table as Jimmy continued his report of the maiden voyage. "I definitely got carried away because I couldn't believe how easy the contraption han**dled.**"

Rick jumped in. "I have two questions. Do you think all three of us can ride in that thing, and where did you find the **fish?**"

Jimmy threw his head back and laughed. "First of all, yes I'm sure it will carry the three of us. Next, there is a huge body of water about a quarter mile from here. The fish are so big that one of them would feed all of us for a couple of m**eals.**"

Glen raised his eyebrows. "We really must figure out how to catch **them.**"

Jimmy didn't hesitate. "I think the best way is to make a raft out of logs, and keep it close to the shore. I don't know what else is in the water, but I didn't see anything **big.**"

Glen smiled. "Then we're going to be having fried fish on a regular basis. We already have three axes to fall trees. We can start t**oday.**"

"Just to finish what I was saying," Jimmy continued, "we can build a big net out of vines. But this is going to be a dangerous proposition, and we need to take all precaut**ions.**"

In no time all three stood on the Riser platform for another test fl**ight.**

With them were guns, ammo, and **axes.**

Showing no apprehension, Jimmy released the pressure valve, starting the main prop. The huge blade spun in earnest, as the men gazed at it, wondering what would ha**ppen.**

It showed plenty of power, and they began rising, even with all the weight. Rick and Glen were astounded, as the machine lifted them higher and hi*gher.*

Jimmy steered in the direction of the water. He sought out the best land route to the shore, in case they couldn't fly back. No carnivores were seen lurking in the woods. Soon the new flying machine soared out and above the w*ater.*

"Wow!" Glen exclaimed as he caught a glimpse of the jumping fish first hand. He slapped Rick and Jimmy's backs exuberantly. "We are going to be feasting **soon!"**

Jimmy couldn't help but smile. "I'm with you man, but right now we'd better get **back."**

Maneuvering a 180 degree turn, he began backtracking, staying high to avoid danger from the gr**ound.**

The jungle below showed no specific path to follow on foot. They would have to inch their way through, hoping to avoid preda**tors.**

As they floated toward home, they watched the ground, and discovered that it was teaming with dangerous looking creatures. What would be the safest way to get there to build the floating plat**form?**

19

CHAPTER

The next morning all three sat around the table nibbling on nuts and ber*ries.*

"This is our quandary." Jimmy opened the conversation. "There's no place to land over by the water, and we can't land on the water. That leaves hiking through the jungle, which is extremely dange*rous."*

Rick popped a nut into his mouth and frowned. "You mean we have to risk our lives going through the jungle, when we could *fly?"*

Jimmy shook his head. "I'd rather fly if there was a place to *land."*

Rick scooted his chair in, and rested his elbows on the table. "I saw a sandy bank that looked big enough to land on. It was down the line, but really a better idea than wal*king."*

"Great!" Glen slapped the table. "I'm not keen on becoming dinosaur fodder either." He grabbed a handful of berries and held it out. "This is good food, but I've got a hankerin' for fish." He popped them into his mouth, and spoke while still chewing. "I figure we need to get in and get out…get this whole thing done in one day. I don't want to stay there any longer than neces*sary."*

Rick signaled a gesture of affirmation. "It's going to be the same as building the wall. Two guys will work, and one will stand guard. Both guns will be near at all t*imes."*

Jimmy nodded his approval. "We'll bring all the ammo and a pile of pre-cut vines. I think we'll need to chop down ten trees for the raft. Make sure their diameters are about ten in*ches."*

"Once this is finished," Rick raised a finger, "I've got a plan to build a fish trap out of bamboo. I think making a net out of vines would be a disa*ster."*

Jimmy shoved back his chair. "So what do you say? Are we ready to get this ***done?"***

Rick and Glen looked grim, but both nodded their heads determin***edly.***

All silently stood and headed up the stairs to the ***deck.***

With the wood heater burning briskly and the tools aboard, the three man crew stepped over the side rail to initiate their jou***rney.***

Jimmy gritted his teeth as he rotated the pressure valve, sending the crew upward. Floating higher into the breeze felt so good that he wished he could just fly around all day. But he had to set his mind on the task at hand. Glen and Rick were thinking along the same lines, and their demeanor showed ***this.***

Jimmy went up extra high just to see more of the land scape. Beyond the river he saw miles of jungle. The other side revealed a vast sea with a distant landscape. This was either an island, or the other side of the ***sea.***

Travelling over the same terrain, the three men looked below and saw teeming animal ***life.***

The higher view revealed several large carnivores in the area. Jimmy shuddered to think of the danger they would face on the ground. To be sure, travelling on foot would be wholly un***wise.***

20

CHAPTER

The Riser travelled slowly toward the water at a higher altitude. Jimmy took note that the pterosaurs didn't fly at such a lofty position. He could see several of them patrolling the skies b*elow.*

As he approached the water, he began a descent toward the shoreline. He strained to focus on the sand bank where he could land. Slowly a spot came into view that appeared good for landing. Jimmy looked at Rick, and pointed to the location. Nodding enthusiastically, Rick cupped his mouth to speak. "That's the *one!"*

Softly the riser lost altitude until it nestled into a tight little space on the sand. Glen and Rick each gripped their weapons, scanning the entire *area.*

"Okay, start chopping trees!" Jimmy barked as though he were a commanding officer. Guns and axes were toted over the side rail, and up the bank. Rick took the first guard duty while Glen and Jimmy each picked a tree. They began swinging with all their might, as though their lives depended o*n it.*

Sweat poured down their faces as they worked. They felt exposed to the dangers of the jungle, but still continued to hack at the trees. Before long, both trees began falling at once. The men stood clear while the trees bounced off the ground. Since they were palm trees, there were no branches to trim *off.*

After cutting the tops off, the men rolled the logs into the water and anchored them with a vine. Glen and Rick then switched places and started on their second pair of *logs.*

Glen kept the fire going in the chamber while Rick and Jimmy worked feveri*shly.*

Jimmy was afraid their presence would attract some unwanted company, and his fears were realized. With no warning, a large carnivore broke through the jungle not ten yards away from him. His reflexes were automatic. In one sweep he dropped the ax and picked up the gun, sliding his finger neatly down to the trigger. He did not attempt to run, but because he was so close, took aim and fired a head shot. The beast only appeared slightly stunned, and quickly became very angry. It roared loudly and started to adv*ance.*

Jimmy then fired the other five shots in rapid succession. As the dinosaur wobbled, he scampered toward the Riser. Rick was already there, but Glen had taken aim, and now fired three shots, which completely stopped the animal. A fierce moaning sound pierced the air, and the giant fell like a tree. After a great thud, all was q*uiet.*

Jimmy and Glen scrambled to reload their weapons. Then they stared at one another, but no one spoke or m*oved.*

21

CHAPTER

At last, Jimmy went back to work on his tree, and Rick followed his lead. They kept a wary eye on the wildlife scavenging the huge carcass. Before long they rolled two more logs into the water.

The work continued that day with no more interruptions. However, plenty of nervous energy was spent grabbing guns at the slightest noise.

When they had collected ten logs, the men grabbed the vines and tightly interlocked them. The result was a sturdy raft that they could land on and fish from. They tied the raft to a jagged rock, making it secure from weather and animals.

The men stood on shore admiring their work. Jimmy threw a fist into the air as a signal of victory. "A good day's work!" He exclaimed. "Let's go home."

They wasted no time getting to the Riser. The fire was stoked, and the chamber pressurized. The prop started spinning, and the craft lifted off the ground.

A sense of relief came over them after risking their lives all day cutting trees. Glen checked out the raft from the air, and envisioned a metal fish trap nailed to one side of it. It would be easy, he thought, to catch fish on a daily basis. A smile cracked his lips.

Jimmy flew high above the usual routes of the pterosaurs. Reaching a good altitude, he leisurely looked out over the ocean. He was suddenly taken back, witnessing a monstrous snake-like beast jumping high out of the water, and gracefully slicing back in. His jaw dropped, and he looked from Glen to Rick. They had both seen it, showing stunned faces. Rick shook his head. "So much for traveling by *boat.*"

Glen laughed. "For sure, flying is the way to go. With something like that in the water, I'll take my chances in the *air.*"

On the way home they saw the usual large numbers of carnivores combing through the jungle. As they approached home, they noticed two large T-Rex looking creatures mulling around just outside the bars. They had somehow flattened the metal spikes on the bottom, to the dismay of all three of the *men.*

With landing of the Riser, the beasts became agitated. They roared and slammed against the bars. Glen jumped over the rail, and ran down the ladder. "Man your weapons quick!" He hollered, as though the others hadn't taken the hint. The men scrambled to the spear guns, trying to avoid sustaining any wall da*mage.*

Each one grabbed a loaded gun, swiveling them around to get clear shots. Both dinosaurs were up against the wall, making it difficult to aim. They grew even more agitated, knowing that their prey was just on the other side of the bars. They became angry and aggressive. Both retreated a few steps, as though gathering momentum for another onsla*ught.*

This was just what Jimmy was waiting for. He took swift aim at the one closest to him, and released the spear. It quickly impaled the carnivore, thrusting clear through to the other side. The beast was stunned, making no sound, and just fell to the ground, lying motion*less.*

Glen took the opportunity to aim and fire at the other marauder. The spear immediately lodged itself into its midsection, and thrust out the other side. In an instant, the cranky raider was silenced, and tumbled to the ground not far from its par*tner.*

22

CHAPTER

Almost immediately, scavengers and smaller wildlife arrived to feed off the carcasses. The men didn't pay any attention, but simply reloaded the spear guns, and trudged into the house. Totally exhausted, they flopped onto their beds, falling asleep almost at *once.*

No one even woke up until the next morning. All three slowly got up and moved around. Glen splashed water on his face from a makeshift faucet on the wall, placed over a metal sink. Bamboo pipes trailed out of the house and all the way down to the cave spring. An ingenious syphoning technique kept constant pressure at the *valve.*

Rick brought shelled coconut and fruit to the table. The fruit resembled a cross between mango and papaya. He sliced three fruits and passed them around to each place at the t*able.*

As they slowly nibbled on the food, they gained en*ergy.*

Rick eyed his roommates before beginning a conversation. "As I said yesterday, there would come a time to build a fish trap. Well, now is the *time.*"

He slurped on a wedge of fruit. "I'll get it done today, and tomorrow we'll be having fried *fish.*"

Glen laughed. "I'm in on this too. In the interest of having fish for dinner, let me know what I can do to *help.*"

"Thanks." Rick seemed delighted. "The concept is very simple. Tie up some bait, like shrimp, inside a bamboo box. Once a fish pulls on the bait, it wiggles the box, which triggers the door to c*lose.*"

Glen nodded and raised his eyebrows. "You may need some metal parts, but even if you don't, I'll help *you.*"

"Okay." Rick smiled and raised two fingers. "I'm going to build two boxes to increase our chances of suc*cess.*"

"Great!" Glen agreed. "Let's get started after break*fast.*"

Jimmy nodded his approval. "While you two are working on the traps, I'll write down as much time travel data as I can remember. Then I can really concentrate on getting us out of this harsh time pe*riod.*"

After breakfast they split up and spent the day at their labors. Rick and Glen joined forces, fine tuning some beautiful bamboo traps with a few metal parts. Rick was confident they would work every time. It took the entire day, but they were certain the result would be more than worth the ef*fort.*

They each carried one trap into the dining room, setting them on the floor. Jimmy sat at the table with a writing utensil and a piece of bark to write on. He eyed the traps, glancing at Rick and Glen, who both smiled. Setting the utensil down, he nodded pleasantly. "You fellows look hu*ngry.*"

$$23$$

CHAPTER

In a jiffy the fire was strong, and the pressure was building. The fish traps were stacked next to the men, as the Riser lifted *off.*

Jimmy and Glen held onto their guns, taking no chances in this barbaric world. The ride over was beautiful, but they held no delusions. The dangerous pterosaurs dominated the sky at lower levels. Jimmy pushed his flying machine straight up as fast as it would go until attaining the proper altitude. They then were able to glide smoothly the rest of the *way.*

Jimmy slowly approached and hovered over the raft. The area seemed clear, so he inched closer and closer, finally touching down on the floating logs. The platform was solid, so he switched off the p*rops.*

Quickly Rick and Glen picked up the traps and carried them to the edge of the raft. They knew exactly what to do. One held a trap to the ends of the logs, while the other drove long nails through holes in the metal. In a few minutes, both traps were secure. Rick then carefully baited and set the traps. He signaled thumbs up as they both scrambled back to the R*iser.*

Jimmy switched the main prop on, causing the rig to tremble and start lifting. He had reached six feet when he noticed two trees along the shore suddenly bending like twigs. His heart skipped a bead at what he saw. All three of the men stood, mouths gaping, staring at a 40 foot tall monster… an obvious carni*vore.*

The mammoth beast caught sight of them, and immediately changed its demeanor. It opened its huge jaws and let out such a blood curdling roar that all three sets of knees in the Riser buc*kled.*

But Jimmy had gripped the pole and remained standing. He pushed the steam wide open, sending them straight up at a faster *clip.*

It didn't appear that they were going to evade the oncoming behemoth, but their ascent suddenly sped up. Jimmy and Rick readied their guns, taking quick aim and firing almost simultaneo*usly.*

As the Riser passed eye level to the goliath dinosaur, the giant lurched forward, opening its jaws, as if to swallow them whole. In desperation, the men each quickly dispatched their remaining three ro*unds.*

The colossal beast looked like an overgrown crocodile standing on it hind legs. Its forward progress was suddenly halted, and it stood there for a few seconds, like a statue. This was just long enough for the Riser to slip up and away, out of its *grasp.*

The men looked down as they floated higher. It was an unforgettable sight. The beast was jumping high in the air, and repeatedly snapping its jaws. It seemed that nothing had ever gotten away from it before, and it was as mad as a ho*rnet.*

Rick shook his head in disbelief, but noticed Jimmy and Glen desperately reloading their guns. Quickly looking up, he saw why. A large pterosaur was rapidly closing in on *them.*

Jimmy handed Rick the gun, shouting, "Shoot him! I have to steer!" Rick suddenly was alarmed at the speed of the great flying beast. It appeared that a collision was immi*nent.*

Raising their weapons at the same time, the two men aimed and fired two rounds apiece. The pterosaur's momentum pushed him directly into the Riser platform. His mouth opened, and a set of sharp teeth bit the edge of the platform before the beast simply dropped straight down and crashed with a thud onto the gr*ound.*

As Rick and Glen looked Jimmy, he wagged his head in disbelief. "Is this really worth going through to catch *fish?"*

24

C H A P T E R

Back home the men rested quietly, each in his own bed. They needed time to recover from this close *call.*

Jimmy frowned as he recalled how twice in a row they had all nearly been killed. They had done their best to build a life of safety in this barbaric *land.*

The time had come for him to really concentrate on time travel. He knew how to make it work, but in a primitive environment, the job would obviously be much more difficult. He thought about each step, and what materials he would need. Mulling it over in his mind, he came up with a list of steps and raw mater*ials.*

After a while Jimmy realized that this was going to be possible. His whole being thrilled with the knowledge that they could get out of this place. It didn't much matter to which time period they went initially, as long as it was one that didn't have dinos*aurs.*

Lying on his back, he put his hands behind his head and looked around. Rick and Glen were both motionless on their beds. Supporting himself with his elbows, he thought for a moment before bouncing to his *feet.*

He walked to the table and took a seat, swiftly writing down the supplies needed to get started. When satisfied, he set the pencil down and smugly nodded to himself. "No reason not to get started at once." He tho*ught.*

Glancing over at Glen, he found that he was now sitting up staring in anticipation. "You look like a man with a plan. You helped to get us into this place. Can you help get us *out?*"

Jimmy's face conveyed determination. His firm lips almost smiled. "If you're willing to lend me a hand, I will get us out of here. That's a pro*mise.*"

The men worked closely together gathering all the materials needed for the project. By the next day their task was comp*lete.*

After a brief discussion about whether to risk checking the fish traps, they came to a consensus. Fish was going to be an important addition to their meager *diet.*

So they bit the bullet, and made another flight to the raft. Jimmy landed, but kept the props going. Glen and Rick each checked a trap, and each came away with a huge fish. They quickly rebaited and jumped back in the Riser. They were headed straight up the instant their feet la*nded.*

Jimmy thought he was going to get away without incident. His altitude was 20 feet when a great commotion occurred on the shore line. Trees were flattened like twigs, as the self-same beast that attacked them before, lunged for*ward.*

"Man your guns!" He shouted, the desperation showing. Glen and Rick were way ahead of him. Each was already aiming, but Jimmy yelled out with some strong advice that sounded like an order. "Shoot his eyes *out!*"

The Riser was escaping upward as fast as possible, but the overgrown walking alligator closed the gap quickly. He jumped high, flying directly up at *them.*

It seemed they were going to be brought down, but Glen and Rick were not going to succumb without a f*ight.*

As the huge jaws drew closer, one eye became an easy target. At about ten feet, both men fired multiple shots at the head, concentrating on the *eye.*

The beast got to within five feet, but its jaw seemed to just flop open. Glen and Rick finished off their rounds as the attacker descended to the ground. They watched it land on its hind feet and stagger for a moment before falling over with a great crash onto the b*each.*

The men said nothing, but only stared at the limp predator b*elow.*

Jimmy shook his head, sizing up the captured *fish.*

25

CHAPTER

The three sat around the table in sober silence, eating fried fish. The long anticipated dinner seemed melodramatic, considering the riskiness of the *catch.*

Jimmy nodded his approval while chewing a big bite. "Getting this fish was tough, but it's going to give us the strength we need to finish the time ma*chine.*"

Rick stared sullenly at Jimmy, slowly chewing the prize fish. A smile crept over his face, and he began to nod. "It's time to get focused on the main issue, and that's to get us out of *here.*"

He leaned forward and spoke more distinctly. "You just make the machine work. Glen and I will take care of everything *else.*"

Glen chuckled as he jabbed another wedge of fish, and stuffed it in his mouth. "You know we'll help though…any way we *can.*"

The next morning found Jimmy absorbed in working magic… exactly as he and the group of scientists had done while working for the government. However, this time it was just just him, and he was in an extremely primitive environ*ment.*

None of this bothered him. He was just as driven, just as riveted in pure concentration. He was living in the past, grasping concepts and principles as they had applied in the earlier construction of the time ma*chine.*

The infrastructure was already in place. Special pipes were already built into the Riser, which allowed for travel into the past and fu*ture.*

These were lower and upper pipes. He knew that the burning of coconut bark releases the agent Benzole, which somehow activated time tr*avel.*

As simple as it sounded, this process had to be micromanaged. The pipes had to be shaped a certain way, and have a certain length. There had to be a separate burning chamber for the coconut *bark.*

Jimmy was on top of all of this. As he worked, his movements were confident and smooth. Lack of resources didn't bother him because he knew how scientific principles applied, and simply adopted *them.*

At day's end, he stood back and looked at his handiwork. He knew it was going to be successful. Glancing behind him, he noticed Glen and Rick standing motionless, viewing his project. They appeared to either be in awe of it, of in total disbelief. He cared not which was the *case.*

Turning around, Jimmy focused on the two bystanders. Hands on hips, he passed his eyes from one to the other. "It's ready for testing. We should not d*elay."*

$$26$$

CHAPTER

The men did not drag their feet on their first time travel test. They gathered the essentials: guns, ammo, food and *water.*

As they stood in the Riser, Jimmy had final words before departure. "We are trying to get back to modern times, but not the exact time from which we came. You know they would probably just send us back here a*gain.*"

Glen looked puzzled. "Do you think this machine will send us to the same geographical area as it moves us into the fu*ture?*"

A nod from Jimmy affirmed the answer. "Yeah, we'll be in the same basic area, but the terrain will be vastly different." He continued as Rick took the hint to start a fire with his flint rock. "Another thing to keep in mind is this. At this point, we don't know how far into the future we'll be headed. It will probably be a trial and error camp*aign.*"

Rick looked up from his flint rock and bark. "It's like I said be*fore.* Anytime will probably be better than this *one.*"

Soon his smoke became flame, and he shared the fire with the logs in the Riser power cha*mber.*

Jimmy turned the shut off valves to the lower smoke pipes, forcing it through the higher pipes. As the coconut bark heated, the benzole spread to the upper wires that wrapped around the Riser. When the benzole concentration grew high enough, the desired effect happened in the surrounding *area.*

The men stood together hanging onto poles and railing tightly. As they looked at the wire perimeter, a vibration started, followed by a buzzing sound. Their view became blurry and distorted. Finally nothing could be seen cle*arly.*

Soon they began feeling dizzy, and lost their sense of position and location. All they could do was to hang on tightly. At about this time, the intensity of this action slowed down, and the dizziness let up. Scenery began to come into view. The land scape was notably very diff*erent.*

Within a couple more minutes, all was still. The three men stood, clutching the Riser framing. No trees or greenery could be seen. They had entered a de*sert.*

Jimmy looked around after silence set in. Within a few seconds he heard noise coming from somewhere. Quickly, he picked up his gun, Glen doing so simultaneo*usly.*

The noise turned into clear footsteps. Facing the source of the noise, they could visualize nothing, seeing that the Riser had landed at the top of a hill. Someone was climbing the side of the hill toward ***them.***

Jimmy swiftly handed his gun to Rick. "I'd better keep my hands on the smoke shutoff va*lves."*

Like statues, Rick and Glen pointed their weapons toward whoever was approaching. Momentarily, they could see heads bobbing, and faces coming into *view.*

A large group of men approached them. They were clad in animal skins, and their hair and beards were long. Most striking of all was their size. Their heights were between 10-12 feet, and their forms were stalky and muscular. They carried swords and spears, bows and ar*rows.*

As soon as they saw the men in the aircraft, they reacted as though under attack. Spreading out, they prepared to fire their wea*pons.*

Alarmed, Jimmy opened the smoke valves. Knowing this would take some time to work, he shouted. "You may have to s*hoot!"*

The giant cave men continued to lurch forward, and one thrust his spear at the Riser. It ricocheted off the rail in front of Rick. He and Glen were shocked, and began shooting at anyone who raised a hand against ***them.***

27

Chapter

Spears and arrows flew past them, but they continued to fire until each of their six rounds were exhausted. Finally the wire around the Riser started vibrating and buz*zing.*

Rick and Glen frantically reloaded. The cave men still charged, and the defenders couldn't finish loading. They aimed and fired at the giant bodies that lunged toward *them.*

As they ran out of ammo again, the wire became a blur. They were forced to grab onto the Riser to keep from falling over. Hanging on for dear life seemed to be a relief, after barely escaping d*eath.*

Within two minutes the blur and instability slowed and stopped. Suddenly a much different picture emerged. A lush, forested terrain surrounded *them.*

All was quiet as the three men relaxed their iron grips on the R*iser.*

Jimmy soon came to his senses. "Better reload quickly. We don't know where we *are."*

Rick and Glen snapped out of their time lags, reloading on the spot. Still everything was serenely quiet. Jimmy stepped over the rail and hopped to the gr*ound.*

The grass was about six inches tall in the clearing. He turned and motioned to the others to follow. Glen and Rick looked each other and jumped to the ground without hesita*tion.*

The group walked across the meadow to a bank of trees. Jimmy pushed aside a few branches, inching forward until another clearing came into *view.*

A strong smell of smoke greeted them. Jimmy peered into the next meadow and found the source. A large group of natives sat and stood around a fire. They wore animal skins, had beads around their necks, and their hair was long. Their general appearance seemed to be Native Ameri*ican.*

As Jimmy stood with Glen and Rick peering over his shoulders, he heard their voices. They were angry, and shouts went back and forth across the *fire.*

Peeking cautiously through the branches, he noticed something else. Each man was equipped with bow and arrow. Each also had tomahawks dangling from their b*elts.*

Jimmy turned and silently slithered back through the trees. Upon returning to the Riser, he leaned against the railing. "We're in danger here." He spoke firmly, but softly. "We're too close to get away cleanly, and I doubt they would accept our friend*ship."*

Rick scowled. "This could end up like the last trip, only we may not be so l*ucky."*

Glen held up his hand. "One thing's for sure. We can't stay **here.**"

Jimmy nodded. "We definitely need to go quite a ways further into the future. We may as well do it **now.**"

Without delay, all three jumped in and manned their stat*ions.*

28

CHAPTER

Jimmy stoked the fire and checked the pipes carefully. As the pressure rose, it found its way through the upper pipes, setting the sequence in mo*tion*.

Then all of them noticed at the same time. A small group of natives came out of the trees, encountering them directly. They appeared quite startled, being mostly women and children. Instantly, they bolted toward the campfire gathe*ring*.

"Better get this thing moving!" Glen sho*uted*.

Jimmy stared at the wires. After what seemed like forever, the action started. Just as a company of warriors barreled through the trees, the Riser started vibrating and buzzing. As the natives raised their weapons, they became blurry and distorted to the crew. Soon nothing could be *seen*.

The time travelers held on tight, knowing they had narrowly escaped death once a*gain*.

As the commotion came to an end, all was still. Jimmy breathed a sigh of relief. Still clutching the pole with one hand, he examined the terrain from one side to the o*ther*.

"Wow!" All three said at once. The Riser was sitting right on a white sandy beach. Ocean waves were rippling up within ten feet of their location. "I don't know where we are," Glen exclaimed, shaking his head, "but this doesn't look like Ame*rica.*"

Above the beach were palm trees, surrounded by thick jungle. The temperature was suddenly warmer, the humidity hi*gher*.

Automatically, Glen and Rick readied their weapons. "The scenery may be lovely," Rick spoke with clenched teeth, "but the natives and animals may not be frie**ndly."**

Jimmy snorted. "So far that has been the **case."**

The men silently looked around, half expecting something or someone to attack **them.**

When nothing happened, Jimmy turned to his two friends. "I've got an idea. Let's take a flight around the area to see what we're going to be contending **with."**

Rick nodded. "That really isn't a bad idea." Reaching into his trouser pocket, he pulled out the flint rock. Squatting next to the furnace, he began striking a rock in the chamber. Within a few minutes, a fire blazed, and he closed the door to build up pres**sure.**

While they waited, the three scoured the horizon. Nothing but sea on one side, and vegetation on the o**ther.**

Soon steam escaped small holes in the pipes, indication the Riser's flight readi**ness.**

Jimmy rotated the pressure valve, causing the main prop to slowly turn. Soon it kicked into high speed, and the Riser began floating up**ward.**

29

C H A P T E R

J immy pulled it up for quite a while, stopping where they would be safe from primitive wea*pons.*

At this height the jungle seemed to have no end. A few small mountains popped up here and there, but mostly flat jungle predomin*ated.*

As he followed the waterfront, Jimmy made a decision to veer left and head in*land.*

"Something tells me this is the way to go." He said, turning to Rick and Glen. "We need to find people, and find out what time period thi*s is.*"

No one had any objections to the course change, and busied themselves with studying the captivating beauty of the ter*rain.*

Palm trees were plentiful, and tropical flowers peppered the landscape. After a few minutes of travel, a clearing appeared. Jimmy squinted at something in the distance. "It's a village! Palm branch huts all over, but where are the pe*ople?*"

"There!" Rick pointed off to the right, where a large crowd of people dressed in animal skins gathered around a great pile of wood. At the top of the pile, tied to a stake, was a young man. "This looks like an execution!" Rick gripped the side r*ails.*

Jimmy scanned the group, and noticed a man stepping toward the stacked wood, holding a torch. Instinctively, Jimmy set a course for the crowd, quickly losing alti*tude.*

The man with the torch suddenly turned around and saw the Riser coming in from about a hundred feet away. The entire crowd now looked up in disbe*lief.*

Men carrying weapons now readied them for action. Some had spears, and some bow & ar*rows.*

Rick and Glen quickly positioned their guns. No one spoke. Without warning, the natives attacked. Arrows and spears bounced off the Riser, some narrowly missing the crew. Neither Glen nor Rick wanted to shoot anyone, but this situation suddenly escalated to survival of the fit*test.*

Glen and Rick fired almost simultaneously at men whose weapons were primed. Neither shot found a live target, but both bounced off a rock wall behind the wood pile. The bullets' impact caused an ear-splitting noise to rip through the *air.*

The Riser was close, and within ten feet of the ground when Rick and Glen saw the warriors' reaction, and fired once more at the rock *wall.*

At this point, fear struck the natives, and they began running away, leaving their weapons be*hind.*

Jimmy drew a deep breath as he lowered elevation to barely touching the ground. "Cut him loose!" He shouted. Glen and Rick jumped out, reaching for home-made knives in their b*elts.*

They swiftly climbed the wood pile and sliced through the cords holding the young man's hands behind his back. He rubbed his wrists, staring at the men who had helped *him.*

Glen bolted back and jumped into the Riser. Rick leaped off the wood pile, turned and looked the youth in the eye. He then beckoned for him to follow, motioning with his hands. "Let's go!" He spoke in earnest. "Come wit*h us!"*

30

C H A P T E R

The young native glanced side to side, finally looking at Rick. Without further delay, he took one step and jumped to the ground, sprinting toward Rick and the Riser. Rick smiled while stepping over the side *rail.*

The tribesman, wearing moccasins and skins, leaped from the ground, literally flying over the rail, landing softly on the floor of the air*craft.*

Jimmy immediately lifted off the ground, speeding straight up. The visitor stood tall, but held on tight. His facial expression showed no fear. He was stoic, even after his close call at the s*take.*

At 200 feet, Jimmy leveled off and headed back toward the beach. This was obviously way too early in his*tory.*

Soon the Riser hovered next to the water, and settled down for a soft landing on the b*each.*

Rick turned and rested a hand on the boy's shoulder. He then patted his own chest, saying "Rick". He tapped himself again, using one finger. *"Rick."*

The young native smiled, pointed at Rick and exclaimed. "Rick!" Laughter and excitement burst from ever*yone.*

Rick then pointed at him, asking, "What is your name?" The young man seemed to be grasping everything. Smiling again, he pointed to himself and said, *"Soto".*

Rick patted his back. "Good". Turning to the others, he introduced them. As he spoke, he pointed. "Jimmy, Glen". Soto then repeated him. "Jimmy, *Glen".*

Jimmy spoke up, as though Soto could understand him. "Right now we must leave. We're going to a different time." He gripped the side rail. "You hold on tight. He glanced at Rick and Glen. "All I can do is keep going forward in time. Can't tell how many years apart each tri*p is.*"

He then turned the prop and pressure chamber valves. The sequence started all over a*gain.*

Everyone stood solemnly gripping the Riser. This continual round of time travel was wearing on them. Soto seemed delighted to have been delivered from death, but the others felt an oncoming sense of despera*tion.*

As the group went through the spin, Soto quietly hung on, showing no sign of fear. As the visual field cleared, a great surprise met them. The Riser was sitting in the center of a village. Not ten feet away sat a great circle of men who appeared to be tribal lea*ders.*

The native leaders did not move, but calmly looked at them and the strange machine that had just appe*ared.*

Rick and Glen nervously gripped their guns, but did not move a mu*scle.*

Suddenly a cry rang out. One man from the circle stood up, spreading his arms in the air as if giving thanks to a higher power. He stepped outside the circle and stopped close to the Riser. A big smile spread over his face. He held out a hand to the men in the Riser, and spoke to them. The three time travelers could understand nothing, but Soto began to *smile.*

$$31$$

CHAPTER

Soto started a conversation with this tribal leader. The older man spoke with great earnestness and expression. Soto seemed to be intimidated at first, but soon was impressed and forthcoming. Their discussion lasted several minutes, at which time the rest of the tribal leaders stood and gathered around the R*iser.*

They exchanged warm greetings with all four, followed by a private chat between Soto and the main le*ader.*

Jimmy noticed something that seemed odd to him. As this leader talked to Soto, he seemed to perceive him as some kind of royalty or d*eity.*

The time travelers were given a hut to stay in, and soon were left alone for the n*ight.*

Jimmy, Rick, and Glen all sat down with Soto, and began to try communicating with him. Their main focus was to get some idea what he and the leader had discu*ssed.*

Being very friendly, Rick went over some language with him, trying to introduce him to English. Progress was made with words like God, Riser, die, and wor*ship.*

A few things became apparent to Jimmy. It seemed the people of this tribe were direct descendants of the ones who tried to kill Soto. They knew the story of Soto's abduction by the strange flying mac*hine.*

Apparently Soto's execution was going to be some kind of sacrifice to their god. The interference by the Riser and abduction of Soto were thought to be divine intervention. That explained why the tribal leaders treated Soto like roy*alty.*

Soto then tried his hardest to get another point across to them. Eventually all understood what he was talking about. The tribal leaders expected their little group to assist them in a conflict with a powerful enemy tribe adjacent to them. Since they were thought of as gods, it was assumed they could successfully defend the weaker t*ribe.*

Jimmy thought about this during the night, as all were bedded down in their hut. He hated the idea of shooting to kill, but they were deeply involved, and had few choices. He decided to not worry about affecting the future. He must deal with events as they occu*rred.*

The next morning, they were given food, and asked to meet the leaders again at the circle. Before heading out, Jimmy spoke with Glen and *Rick.*

"We are going to have to defend this tribe as they have asked us t*o do."*

Rick gave a half smile, and shook his head. "The only advantages we have are these two guns with limited ammo. I have no idea how we're going to accomplish *this."*

Jimmy looked at Glen. "Well, if you can scrape up some iron, I have some i*deas."*

Glen's eyes twinkled. "Now you're talking sense. We can make some decent weapons with *iron."*

Rick tapped a finger on Jimmy's chest. His eyebrows curled as he spoke. "Would it be possible to build a more powerful Riser that has metal siding for protec*tion?"*

Jimmy slowly grinned. "The answer is yes. It will be well protected and well defe*nded."*

Glen patted Jimmy's shoulder. "We'll scout around for iron ore t*oday.* I'll go start the fire *now."*

32

CHAPTER

The time travelers approached the circle where the tribal leaders were seated. When he saw them coming, the apparent chief stood. He smiled and beckoned the group **over.**

Approaching Soto, he began speaking in earnest. Soto nodded repeatedly, saying a few words in agree**ment.**

As the chief's words came to an end, Soto turned to Jimmy. He used sign language in an attempt to relay the message. It didn't take long to get the point across. There was a large army on the other side of the valley. The chief wanted them to fly over the jungle and drive them **away.**

Jimmy stepped forward, attempting to communicate with both the chief and Soto. He indicated that he would make the trip over the jungle, but that he needed time to build a larger and more powerful flying mac**hine.**

When the chief insisted that something must be done now, Jimmy agreed to an immediate mission using the existing aircraft. He led the way to the Riser, followed by Rick. Glen now had the fire roaring. Soto said something to the chief, after which the tribal leader barked an order to a group of his soldiers. Someone quickly produced a bow with a large quiver of arrows. Soto then ran like lightening to the side rail, leaping over it with **ease.**

Jimmy started the upward climb without delay. The four men rose higher and higher to about 200 **feet.**

The entire tribe stood below gazing up at them, and marveling at the s**ight.**

Jimmy set a course over the jungle to see what they were up against. Turning to his compatriots, he shook his head. "I don't know what to tell you gentlemen, but we are going to keep a high enough altitude to stay out of da*nger.*"

"We'd better." Rick retorted. "We are no match for an army." "This should be just a scouting mission." Glen chippe*d in.*

"You're right." Jimmy conceded. We should see how many of them there are, and how aggressive they *are.*"

Beneath them were groves of palm trees filled in with thick jungle. One or two large elephant looking creatures were seen amidst it all. These, apparently, were masto*dons.*

The Riser floated along at 200 feet, and was silent except for the rotating blade above. The jungle seemed to carry on much longer than anticip*ated.*

Soto stood stoically, his bow primed with an arrow. Much to Jimmy's delight, there were no large predators in the air. What existed on the ground still remained to be *seen.*

Soto's eye caught something off to one side. Pointing excitedly, he spoke a newly learned word. *"See!"*

The others noticed immediately that something was different about the jungle pattern. Jimmy turned about and set a course to the left. Soon they glided directly over a large trail carved out of the thick growth. Peering to the left, they saw two men with stone hatchets cutting away the vines and small t*rees.*

$$33$$

Chapter

The brush cutters saw them right away, and ran into the forest as if they'd seen a *ghost.*

Jimmy ignored them, and veered to the right in order to follow the trail to its so*urce.*

The men in the aircraft gripped their weapons nervously. The Riser flew straight along the freshly cut growth. No one else was in sight, and the trail went on for quite a dist*ance.*

Before long Soto noticed a large clearing ahead. He pointed while excitedly talking in his own language. Everyone then noticed a group of soldiers running toward them down the path. The Riser had been *seen.*

They were still too high for spears or arrows to reach them, but the warriors below tried anyway. No weapon came even half the distance needed to threaten *them.*

Jimmy calmly glided along the pathway and into the clearing. There he discovered the main camp. People below were frantically running around and pointing skyward. Jimmy wondered to himself if they too had heard the story of Soto's deliver*ance.*

He flew until he had a good picture of the enemy's strength and numbers. He estimated a thousand soldiers compared to his ally's 100 *men.*

A large company of archers continued to follow the Riser, launching arrows that came nowhere near their tar*gets.*

Jimmy set a course for home, having gained all the information he needed. Not one minute had passed when Soto suddenly yelled "Latanna!" He pointed and continued shou*ting.*

Jimmy, Rick, and Glen all looked back at the same time. They were startled to see a large dinosaur stalking the natives. It looked similar to some of the predators they had seen earlier in *time.*

"I can't believe it!" Rick muttered. "I thought we were way past this." Instinctively, he turned the Riser around to travel toward the b*east.*

The soldiers had gathered together, and were now attacking the great carnivore. Everyone watched helplessly, as arrows and spears simply bounced off the thick *skin.*

The soldiers began backing away from the dinosaur, who lunged repeatedly at them. The huge jaws snapped sharply just above their heads. Their weapons were like toys against such an e*nemy.*

Jimmy had seen enough. Hovering over the attacking creature, he descended slowly. "Try and get some good shots!" He yelled at Rick and Glen. They raised their guns, but before they could fire, Soto launched an arrow. It struck and sunk deeply into one of the monster's eyes. It shook its head violently, and roared loudly. Rick and Glen took this as a clue. They both pasted the man-eater with bullet after bu*llet.*

It made an attempt to come after the Riser, but leaned heavily to one side, and fell to the gr*ound.*

34

C H A P T E R

All the soldiers and villagers cheered, pumping their fists into the air. Jimmy took the lead by waving at them. "Do what I do!" He shouted. Rick and Glen quickly joined in. Soto seemed confused, but followed suit, waving at the *crowd.*

Jimmy did not want to risk landing on the ground, so he flew back toward the forest, waving the whole time. This, he thought, might at least delay an attack by the larger t*ribe.*

Rick patted Soto on the back. "Good shot!" He grinned and pointed to the bow. Soto smiled and no*dded.*

A few minutes later the Riser drifted over the smaller village. All the people stood around waiting for them impatie*ntly.*

As Jimmy touched down, the chief approached with an inquisitive look on his *face.*

Stepping to the ground, Soto and Jimmy seemed confident and happy. Soto knew the chief's question before he asked it. He began explaining the substance of their journey, including the dinosaur attack, as he went through the motions of using a bow and a*rrow.*

The chief's expression bore surprise and amazement. He glanced from one to another of the tribal leaders who were standing nearby. Looking back at Soto and Jimmy, he placed a hand on each one's shoulder. He declared something which Jimmy couldn't understand, and strutted away, clapping his hands while talking to the lea*ders.*

Hoping things would settle down now, Jimmy signaled for the others to return to the hut with *him.*

With everyone inside, they tried to relax and unwind. Jimmy sat on the floor and leaned against the wall. The others followed *suit.*

Placing his arm on a shelf, he smiled confidently. "We still need to look for iron deposits. When we find a good one, we are going to build a steam powered helicopter. It uses a high pressure steam chamber, which generates unbelievable power." He paused for a moment. "This little flying machine has served us well, but we've been lucky. We need something safer, faster, and stro*nger."*

Glen perked up. "I didn't know you could go that high tech! Where was the helicopter when we nearly got devoured all those t*imes?"*

Rick laughed. "Under the circumstances, he did pretty *well."*

Jimmy nodded. "And they still have dinosaurs here. I really think we should build an iron fence around this village first t*hing."*

"Correction." Rick interjected. "_We_ will build an iron wall. _You_ can work on the helicopter." He placed a hand on Soto's shoulder. "He can talk the villagers into helpin*g us."*

"Very well." Jimmy sounded impressed. "We'll rest a bit, then go scouting for *iron."*

A half hour later the group was in the air again. Jimmy headed for the rocks to get a clear view of any iron depo*sits.*

Far above the rocky slopes, the Riser glided. Jimmy noticed some indentations along the slope. Lowering his altitude, he could see a group of caves clumped together. As he got lower, he positively identified red rock in and around the c*aves.*

"That's what we're looking for!" He exclaimed, slapping the main pole with *gusto.*

35

C H A P T E R

That night in their hut, the men rested as they ate fruit and nuts. Glen threw a handful of nuts into his mouth, motioning to Jimmy. "That iron ore out there is all I need. We'll just start hauling baskets of it back here in the R*iser.*"

Jimmy nodded. "I agree, but still the most important thing is safety. We must build a wall around this village first. Then we'll be safe from attack by man or b*east.*"

"Sounds right." Rick went along. "Then we can take our time building the next Riser, and do it r*ight.*"

The next day was a great start indeed. Jimmy landed by the cluster of caves, and Glen verified that the iron ore was high qua*lity.*

Work started immediately. The one pic they brought was put to *use.*

The soft ore crumbled easily, and the men made several trips a *day.*

After a week the fence began taking shape, which caused quite a stir among the villagers. Many stepped in to help in the construc*tion.*

Glen sped up the iron making process, and within one month the fence around the village was done. The natives, who had never seen iron before, believed this to be some kind of miracle. They were so ecstatic to have protection from the large predators, that they had celebrations every night. They were unafraid to make fires at night, and have noisy par*ties.*

But the time travelers went to bed early, and worked hard all day. Jimmy now turned his attention to building the new Riser. He worked closely with Glen, who followed instructions for the shaping of p*arts.*

Rick and Soto helped, but during their down time they could always be seen studying the English language. Soto increased his vocabulary as time went *by.*

After four months, Jimmy finally pronounced his project complete. It resembled a flying disc with no top. It was made of light wood and bamboo covered with a layer of metal. Like the first Riser, it had a main support pole with a very large prop on top, and a smaller directional prop that swiveled manu*ally.*

The time transport mechanism was much more detailed and developed than the first one. The two fire chambers were much larger and well built. Several holes just big enough to fire a weapon through were spaced along the floor. Jimmy had not tested flight or time travel yet, but all was made according to the specifications he rememb*ered.*

On this particular morning the time travelers stood next to the Riser. All around were crowds of people anxious to see the new machine te*sted.*

36

Chapter

The crew stood in the expansive new Riser ready for a test flight. The fire chamber was primed and ready. Tribesmen stood surrounding the craft, buzzing with excite***ment.***

Jimmy glanced at his companions, and slowly released pressure at the valve. At once the huge prop turned, increasing rpms rap***idly.***

In no time, Riser 2 was lifting off the ground, smooth and easy. The crowd buzzed with energy, as they pointed, laughed, and cla***pped.***

All four passengers became engrossed in this new and gentle way of fl***ying.***

Jimmy wanted to test the limits of his new invention, so he went straight up as fast as possible. The crew felt like they were aboard a rocket blasting off. Riser 2 was quick and a***gile.***

At about 200 feet, Jimmy stopped, grabbed the secondary prop handle, and sent them straight ahead at a much faster clip than Riser 1 could go. Then after testing a few maneuvers, he descended back to earth. As the craft gently touched ground, the natives cheered and cla***pped.***

Jimmy turned to Glen and Rick. "Let's travel forward in time as far as we can. This is as good a time as ***any."***

Rick nodded. "I hope you know what you're d***oing."***

Glen threw some coconut bark into a special heating chamber. It was already stoked with wood, and began burning right away. A couple minutes later, smoke entered the higher pipes. A force field developed all around the Riser, causing obscured vision, and mild shuddering. Within two minutes their sight was totally hindered, and all were stricken with dizziness. Then a boom was heard, and vision became clear a*gain.*

Everyone breathed deeply as they looked around. Houses made of brick and shale lined a dirt road. Horses were tied to railings outside the homes. Riding and walking through the streets were what appeared to be Mexican cowboys of the 1*800s.*

Suddenly the Riser shook again, and the vision became obscured. The men grabbed onto the side rails, as without warning, they were sent reeling into another time *zone.*

Again the spinning stopped, and the scene cleared up. In front of them appeared a world that none had ever seen or dreamed of. Futuristic sky scrapers towered all around. Shockingly, people flew in midair with no clear power source. Jimmy put his hand to his mouth in unbe*lief.*

Just as quickly, they were thrown into a spin again. All were forced to hang on. What was happening? This machine had spiraled out of con*trol!*

37

CHAPTER

As the horizon cleared, a wide view of the ocean stood before them. Salt air purged their nostrils. Looking around, Jimmy noted the Riser sat 50 yards from the shore. Just behind them was a wild looking jungle. The air was warm and m*uggy.*

Half expecting to be whisked away to another time, all hung on t*ight.* No one moved or spoke for a mo*ment.*

Then Jimmy exhaled, slowly releasing his grip on the prop pole. "Looks like we're staying for the time b*eing."*

Rick flashed a concerned look at Jimmy. "What the hell is going on with this mac*hine?"*

Jimmy shook his head. "I'm going to have to trouble shoot it. There's something affecting smoke flow in the p*ipes."*

Glen snorted. "I think that's a given, but is this the best place to work on it? Looks a bit prehistoric *here."*

"Oh, I agree." Jimmy glanced nervously from side to side. "But I'm almost afraid to try time travelling right now. What if it doesn't stop switchin*g us?"*

He knelt down and began an examination of the lower p*ipes.*

Soto looked suspiciously around the jungle. Many sounds were escaping from its depths. Rick and Glen nervously raised their weapons, scanning the terrain. Soto reached into his quiver and pulled out an a*rrow.*

Jimmy ran a wire into the pipes, after which he blew into each *one.*

He then repeated the process on the upper p*ipes.*

In the distance, a deep-throated roar ominously sounded. Then an answer came from another beast. Momentarily, a great commotion commenced. Branches snapped, and rocks crashed. Angry bellows and roars pierced the *air.*

Jimmy unflinchingly labored to clear the pipes. Rick glanced at Jimmy. "We got to get out of here! You ready to try it *yet?"*

Jimmy suddenly stood, heaving a great sigh. "Okay, let's do it!" He yelled. Quickly, he turned the shut-off valve, and then the pipe valve, forcing smoke into the upper p*ipes.*

Huge crashes shot out from the jungle, followed by trees falling. Directly ahead of them emerged a towering figure. Its height appeared to be around 30 feet. The massive predator stood still for a moment, cocking its head to one *side.*

While hearts were skipping a beat, the behemoth raised his head to the sky and nearly split everyone's ear drums with a spine tingling blast from its th*roat.*

Rick and Glen were so badly shaken that they could hardly raise their guns. But they did aim and fire repeat*edly.*

The great meat eater swayed backward a little, but quickly recovered. Rick and Glen frantically reloaded, dropping bullets on the floor because their hands shook so b*adly.*

This really angered the giant dinosaur. It lunged forward and leaned down to snatch the Riser between its jaws. By this time Jimmy's machine had started the motion process. The Riser actually slammed into the huge head, infuriating it even *more.*

But the men cut loose with another barrage of bullets at close range. Visibly, holes were being ripped into the colossal brute's face. As the scene became distorted, the men saw a fading picture of the monster succumbing, and falling back*ward.*

38

CHAPTER

As the turbulence dwindled, a new world came into view. To their surprise and wonderment, it appeared to be the same futuristic scene that had so quickly passed them by earlier. Peaceful palaces and sky scrapers dominated, and people were magically flying all around, aided by an unknown power so*urce.*

As the four men viewed this beautiful and apparently blissful place, a loud voice from behind them barked out an order. "Hands up, and drop your wea*pons!"*

A group of police with strange looking guns quickly surrounded them. The time travelers could do nothing else, so they comp*lied.*

The man with the loud voice stepped to the front. "Everyone down here now!" On cue, they all climbed over the rail and jumped to the ground. They stood before a man with a fat head, pudgy nose, and an odd, space-age uni*form.*

The military leader paced in front of the time travelers, eyeing each one suspicio*usly.*

"You'd better tell me the truth!" He thrust his chin into the air as he spoke. "Where are you from, and what are you doing *here?"*

Jimmy looked at his comrades before he spoke. "We are time travelers from your *past."*

The man's eye narrowed and his round face reddened. "I gave you a chance to tell the truth! Now you'll have to pay the price!" He lifted his rifle and pointed it at J*immy.*

"Stop!" An authoritative voice came from a distance. The pudgy Sergeant stiffly turned around and saw his commanding officer standing at the top of the *hill.*

"Lower your weapon!" The officer ordered. He then came bounding down the hill. The sergeant's face turned red, and he shouldered his *rifle.*

As the officer approached, his eyes were glued to the Riser. Coming to a stop, he studied Jimmy. "I'm Colonel Bishop. Did I hear you say you are from the *past?"*

Jimmy stood erect, looking the colonel straight in the eye. "My name is Jimmy Brooks, and you heard correctly. We are time trave*lers."*

The colonel seemed to pause for a moment, unable to hold back a slight grin. He offered his hand for Jimmy to shake. "I'd like to speak with you. Follow me. Your machine will be guarded, so don't worry abou*t it."*

He turned and began walking…a handful of soldiers following along. Jimmy started out, motioning for the others to come a*long.*

Colonel Bishop walked next to Jimmy and his group. The soldiers kept pace, carrying, but not pointing their *guns.*

The colonel led them along a sidewalk that turned into steps leading up a hill. At the top it leveled off and went in a straight line toward a large building. Pointing at the building, he spoke to Jimmy. "My office is on the first f*loor."*

Guards at the door saluted the colonel. He returned the salutes, and led the way through the *door.*

39

CHAPTER

He walked down a narrow hallway, and suddenly stopped, opening a door on the right. He glanced at the time travelers. "Come in and find a seat." Turning his attention to the soldiers, he fired an order. "Wait out **here.**"

As the group sat in cushioned chairs, the colonel closed the door. He stepped behind a desk and sat down. Folding his hands, he smiled as he spoke. "Let me guess. You are from somewhere between 2035 and **2050.**"

Jimmy raised his eyebrows. "Yes, 2040, but how did you **know?**"

Colonel Bishop smiled. "That's the only period of active time tr**avel.** After that, it was declared illegal, and the technology was **lost.**"

The colonel paused and scratched his face as if deep in thought. He continued. "A friend of mine has devoted his life to rediscovering the art of time travel. His name is professor Jennings. I really would like you to meet **him.**"

Jimmy nodded. "I would be happy to talk to him. By the way, may I ask what year thi**s is?**"

The colonel laughed. "I'm sorry. I assumed you knew. It's 2280." Mouths gaping, the time travelers looked at one ano**ther.**

Colonel Bishop sat straight in his chair. "At any rate, I want you to know that if you will show professor Jennings the technology, you will be given everything you need. You'll be living **well.**"

Jimmy smiled. "We'll accept that **deal.**"

Clapping his hands in delight, colonel Bishop grinned and nodded. "I can take you to his office right **now.**"

Jimmy held up a hand. "That's fine, but time travel is my responsibility. Would you mind setting my friends up with living accommod*ations?*"

"Absolutely! The colonel answered enthusiastically. "Follow me right this way." Standing, he led his visitors down the hallway again. After a short distance, he ducked into an office. "Suzy, set these men up with a four bedroom place, pl*ease.*"

Jimmy waved to his friends as he followed the colonel. "I'll find you" were his parting words, as he rushed to keep *pace.*

Colonel Bishop led him back outside to a parking lot, and approached a new car. Turning to Jimmy, he opened what looked like an ink pad. "Place one thumb on this pad." Jimmy complied, pressing his right thumb on the pad. Out popped a plastic card. "Grab the card." The colonel seemed to be issuing orders as though Jimmy were a sol*dier.*

Jimmy didn't let this bother him, as he quickly pulled the card from the mac*hine.*

The colonel smiled. "That will get you into the car. It now belongs to *you.*"

Jimmy blinked, and raised his eyebrows in surp*rise.*

Colonel Bishop wasted no time. "Follow my car. It's parked just over there." He turned and marched *away.*

Quickly, Jimmy slid the card to unlock the door, and got in to study how to turn on the engine. He found the start button with no difficulty, and fired it up. Easing forward, he followed the col*onel.*

40

CHAPTER

Colonel Bishop pulled up to a large new looking building. Stopping directly behind him, Jimmy powered down the engine and stepped out of the car. He couldn't help but stare at hundreds of people flying about 20 feet above the road, and following the traffic ro*utes.*

He quickly followed the colonel into the building, and up to the 10th floor. The men stepped off the streamline elevator and down the hall to a lavish office with the name "Professor Tom Jennings" on the *door.*

Behind a desk sat a man appearing to be around 40 years of age. He had bushy black hair and a pronounced must*ache.*

"Tom," the colonel blurted out, "I'd like you to meet som*eone."*

As Tom looked up, the colonel forged ahead. "This is Jimmy Brooks from the year *2040."*

Immediately, Tom's attention was riveted on J*immy.*

He directed his gaze back to Colonel Bishop. "Come again?" He stood, eyes wide with anticipation. He didn't wait for the colonel's resp*onse.*

"So you are a time traveler!" Jimmy nodded hesita*ntly.*

Tom pressed his lips together as he marched around the desk, and held out his hand. With a quick handshake, he gestured with his other arm. "Please, have a *seat."*

"I'll see you later, Jimmy. Got to go." The colonel disappeared, leaving Tom and Jimmy facing each o*ther.*

Tom forced a laugh. "I have no idea where the colonel found you, but he knows I've been trying to glean information about time travel for y*ears."*

He pulled up a chair and sat, folding his hands as if trying to calm his nerves. "Look," he smiled as he spoke, "I hope you'll discuss what you know about time travel technology with me. It would mean a great deal t*o me.*"

Jimmy nodded. "Yes, I can tell you just about anything you want to know." He paused briefly. "I just need security for me and my friends. You know, a job and a place to **stay.**"

Tom laughed heartily. "Believe me, you'll have much more than that if you can help me learn to navigate **time.**"

Jimmy leaned back in his chair, nodding his head. Looking squarely at Tom, he smiled. "All I want to do is stay here. If you knew where I've spent the last several months, you would unders**tand.**"

Tom held out his hand again. "Sounds to me like we have a deal!" Jimmy smiled as he shook. "Yes, w**e do.**"

"By the way," Tom queried, "just where did you spend the last several mo**nths?**"

The answer came with a scowl. "Fighting dinosaurs in the cretaceous pe**riod.**"

Tom's eyes widened, and his jaw g**aped.**

Jimmy continued. "I was sent there on a false murder conviction. I met Rick and Glen there, and together we mined iron ore. We build a metal wall, giving us safety until I could get the time machine b**uilt.**"

Tom seemed speechless, just sitting there shaking his head. He finally came around. With some effort, he spoke. "I want to go back to that time and see what it was **like.**"

Jimmy's eyes narrowed. "No you d**on't.**"

41

Chapter

"**I**s there a specific reason," Jimmy queried, "why you're interested in time tr*avel?*"

Tom smiled. "Nothing specific. I've just always been interested in the sub*ject.*"

He pointed a finger at Jimmy. "Ever since I learned about your brief history of government controlled time travel, I've been fascinated by it I've been experimenting for years, but never really made any prog*ress.*"

He looked straight at Jimmy. "Would you work with me in my lab, and show me how it's ***done?***"

"Sure." Jimmy nodded. "But let me tell you up front. We should build it inside an air craft. One that moves vertically, and that has powerful wea***pons.***"

Tom thought for a moment. "I've got just what we need for that." He hinted a grin. "Well, really, Colonel Bishop has it. It's a jet fighter that lands and takes off without a runway. It holds up to ten people, and uses solar p***ower.***"

"That is precisely what we need." Jimmy affirmed. "And I do look forward to helping you. But I would like to get some sense of your ambitions for time travel. If it's really just curiosity, give me an example of where you want to go, and ***when.***"

Tom cradled his chin with one hand, thinking hard. He turned his gaze to Jimmy, raising his eyeb***rows.***

"I'd like to find out just what killed off the dinosaurs. I'd like to enhance our knowledge of his***tory.***"

Jimmy tried to disguise a scowl. "Really, I just came from there, and vowed never to return." After a pause, he continued. "Hundreds of men were killed by dinosaurs after being sent there totally unprep*ared.*"

Tom shook his head. "I didn't realize that. If we travel there, we'll take all safety precaut*ions.*"

"That's why I wouldn't do it without plenty of weapons." Jimmy sounded unenthusiastic. "I'm not worried about being able to get there. I'm worried about staying a*live.*"

Tom held up one hand. "I get it, but we'll give ourselves every advantage. Don't you think it'll be worth it for the kind of lifestyle you'll be living here? Believe me, you won't be able to bea*t it.*"

"Alright." Jimmy conceded. "All I ask is that I have a say in construction of *this.*"

"Absolutely." Tom heartily agreed. "In fact, the project is yours. I simply want to be there to l*earn.*"

"Great." Jimmy couldn't hold back a smile. "The first thing to do is get that fancy jet into a warehouse. We'll set up the time machine in the airc*raft.*"

Tom stood, checking his watch. "It'll be there by tomorrow. R i g h t now let me show you where you'll be sta*ying.*"

Jimmy sprang to his feet and followed *Tom.*

42

Chapter

Stopping at a tidy looking house in a residential area, Tom got out of his car and walked back to Jimmy, who stepped out of *his.*

"This is your place." He smiled. "Hope it satisfies *you.*"

Jimmy snorted. "After cowering in a cave to keep away from dinosaurs, I'm sure just about anything would be *fine.*"

With a smirk on his face, Tom patted Jimmy's shoulder. "I'll come and pick you up tomorrow. We'll get started on the pro*ject.*"

As Tom drove off, Jimmy sighed. Stepping slowly up to his new quarters, he thought of how great it was going to be to just relax and live luxuriously, at least in comparison to the recent *past.*

The front door was unlocked, and as it swung open, a flavorful aroma of cooked food met *him.*

Glen stood at the oven holding a spatula, and Rick was conversing with Soto on the *couch.*

"Hey, just in time for dinner!" Glen sounded jovial, as he scurried about the kitchen. "This is a pretty nice place, and they gave us money for grocery shop*ping.*"

Jimmy appeared weary, but looked around with admiration. "We won't know how to handle such comfort." He joked, setting his car card on the counter, and heading for a soft c*hair.*

As he sat down, he noticed how spirited the conversation was between Rick and Soto. Rick had been working hard tutoring him in English, and now it was paying *off.*

Seeing Jimmy, Soto addressed him, showing off his new language skills. "I have decided to work with you building the time mac*hine.*"

His eyes sparkled, and Jimmy could tell he felt great sincerity. Put on the spot, he was taken back for just a moment. He offered a pleased nod. "That is good news! I could use your help. We will be starting tomo*rrow.*

Soto flashed a grinned, appearing so thrilled that he could hardly stay seated. "I will do anything to help. I do want to learn if you would teac*h me.*"

Jimmy gestured with his arm. "Yes! I'll be teaching professor Jennings, so you can both learn toge*ther.*"

Rick scooted forward on the couch. "Just so you know, Glen and I only want regular jobs. We're done with time tr*avel.*"

Jimmy slapped his knee. "In a way, that's how I feel. But it's the time machine that's buying our tickets to success right now. I have to stick wit*h it.*"

43

CHAPTER

The next morning at 9am, Tom arrived. Jimmy answered the door and invited him in for a moment. "This is Soto, who we found in the ancient past. He's done well studying conversational Eng*lish.*"

Tom was astounded at this, and shook Soto's hand. "Any idea what year you're from?" He looked at Soto, then at J*immy.*

"Well, we know dinosaurs still ruled." Jimmy offered with a half s*mile.*

"I am happy to live here now." Soto sounded sincere. "It was very hard and very dangerous where I came *from.*"

Jimmy placed one hand on Soto's shoulder as he spoke. "Soto wants to observe and learn as we work. I hope it presents no problem to *you.*"

Tom's thick moustache disguised a smile. "Absolutely." He patted Soto's arm. "We can learn toge*ther!*"

The three men rode in Tom's car to a large warehouse not far away. Pulling into a parking spot that read "Professor Jennings", Tom spoke. "Here we are! The aircraft is in*side.*"

As he stepped out of the car, Jimmy noticed the surrounding area seemed deserted. "Not much going on around here." He comme*nted.*

Tom smugly looked straight ahead as he walked. "That's for a pur*pose.* I don't want publicity, at least until the project is fini*shed.*"

He suddenly stopped and turned, grasping Jimmy's arm. "We've got government support here. Jimmy, we can use whatever resources we need. This job is going to be first c*lass.*"

Jimmy was surprised at this positive and unexpected declaration. He seemed mesmerized by Tom's thick eyebrows and mustache. He blinked twice, and met Tom's gaze. "Well, I'll have to expand my thinking if we're going to have some high quality equipment to work *with.*"

Tom nodded. "That's how I want you to see it. We're going to stay safe, no matter what time period we trave*l to.*"

The scientists then strolled up to the warehouse door, and opened it. It revealed nothing but darkness, until Tom reached in and flipped the light*s on.*

A flash of silver reflected brightly into their eyes. Jimmy held a hand over his face, then let it go, squinting heavily. His eyes adjusted to the view. A massive jet fighter was sitting triumphantly just in front of *them.*

He stood staring in admiration, not able to speak. Soto took it in, his mouth gaping. He had never taken in such a s*ight.*

Tom stepped forward, spreading his arms as he looked at Jimmy. "You'll just have to think on a larger scale." He smiled, as he moved closer to study Jimmy's face. "That won't stop you, wil*l it?*"

Jimmy lifted his head, and gently wagged it. "No, it w*on't*".

44

CHAPTER

The first day was a sensory overload for Soto, who had lived his entire life in a primitive environment. He followed Jimmy and Tom around, feeling too ignorant to ask questions. But at the same time, he was fascinated, and his attention was riveted on everything that was said or **done.**

Tom took notes from the start, knowing that he had experimented for so long unsuccessfully. He was even more enamored with the proceedings than **Soto.**

Jimmy first examined the aircraft, studying how he could place time travel technology therein. He was pleased with the spacious 10 passenger c**abin.**

Over the next two weeks, he found that Tom's research had not been that far off. He had used coconut bark as the active agent, but did not distribute the smoke effecti**vely.**

Jimmy then found by conducting laboratory experiments, that he could pre-harvest the enzyme from the bark. He then could get much better mileage out of it in a way that didn't require a constant bark **fire.**

The three men would sit for a conference at the start of each day. Jimmy would explain what he planned for that day, and answer any questions posed by Tom or Soto. Then they would go to work, actually doing what they had discu**ssed.**

Everything was done state-of-the-art. No cost was sp**ared.**

Jimmy's biggest challenge was including the entire aircraft in the transport field. But he and Tom together found the solution. They were successful in spreading the enzyme over the plane's surface, having a built-in supply that would last for long periods of *time.*

After three months of intense work on the project, it was completed. Tom then arranged special flight training to be done before testing the time travel sy*stem.*

All three were enrolled in an intense flight school for two more months. Each practiced take off, flying, and landing until their skills were sharp. Classroom studies were a part of the daily co*urse.*

At last they had triumphed in science and training. They were ready to test their *work.*

45

C H A P T E R

om, Jimmy, and Soto sat around a table in the warehouse kitchen sipping coffee. A feeling of anticipation prevailed as Tom poured creamer and sugar into his cup. As he stirred, he looked from Jimmy to Soto. "This is the day." He smiled as he raised his cup, taking a hefty swig. "I'd like to go back to the Cretaceous period, and then move forward from t*here.*"

Jimmy's reaction was less than enthusiastic. "If you're planning to walk around on the ground, you're going to want something with more power than an elephant gun." He slowly stirred his drink. "I won't go unless we ge*t it.*"

As Soto nodded in agreement, Tom was already answering. "That's already taken care of. The weapon is a super caliber air gun. On its highest setting, it will penetrate any flesh…even the toughest *hide.*"

Jimmy grinned slightly. "It hasn't been tested on dinos*aurs.*"

With a nervous laugh, Tom replied. "Of course not, but I would wager that it would do the *job.*"

"Well," Jimmy took a sip, "we had better try it from a safe dist*ance.*"

Tom pulled his chair back, and placed an ankle over his knee. "Then we'll leave this afternoon as pla*nned.*"

The men spent a couple of hours at the range shooting air rifles. Jimmy was duly impressed with the devastation this weapon caused. And it was so light, it felt like a *toy.*

Soto laughed while he blasted a hole through two layers of metal sheeting. "This would kill any beast, I don't care how *big!*"

Jimmy chuckled softly. "Don't be too confident. Never be too confi*dent.*"

That afternoon the trio met on the blacktop surrounding the warehouse. The big jet almost looked defiant, as they approached. Jimmy opened a door on the belly of the plane, and pulled out a folding ladder. He climbed up without hesitation, and the others followed quickly after him. Jimmy navigated a steep stairway, and emerged into the spacious cockpit. He walked down an aisle separating two rows of seats. Reaching the pilot's chair, he sat while flipped switches and pushed but*tons.*

Tom buckled into the copilot's seat while Soto secured himself into a seat behind *them.*

Jimmy's gaze then landed on Tom. "You simply want to visit the Cretaceous period, as I re*call.*"

"That's correct." Tom spoke with confidence. "We'll get into the air first, and then make the time transi*tion.*"

Jimmy nodded, still reluctantly going along with the plan. "There's no other way we can do this safely." He punched in coordinates on a keyboard. After manipulating some controls on the instrument panel, he looked at Tom and spoke. "Here w*e go.*"

46

Chapter

The big engine hummed eerily for a few seconds before Jimmy initiated a soft liftoff. Up they went, straight to the sky. He hovered for another few seconds before activating the time travel sequence, which was pre-progra*mmed.*

Tom and Jimmy made eye contact. Here was the moment of t*ruth.*

Would the time machine actually **work?**

Suddenly they felt a quivering motion, accompanied by a hazy appearance outside. Then a faint boom was heard, followed by normal engine s*ound.*

All three men eagerly peered out the window. They were not disappointed. Below they saw a forest of prehistoric trees. With a little scanning of the horizon, they quickly saw them…creatures of all kinds. Most obvious were the big ones: monstrous Brontosauruses feeding on the treetops. Also visible were large meat eaters scouring the land for potential *prey.*

Tom was entranced by the all too realistic sight. He took a deep breath, exhaling slowly. While he was silent, Jimmy moved along slowly, keeping high enough to avoid da*nger.*

New sights came into view: creatures large and small, many of them unfami*liar.*

After a protracted period of time, Jimmy broke the silence. "So you wanted to see what killed the dinosaurs. We should move forward in time to look for any cha*nges."*

Tom nodded emphatically, as if suddenly coming out of a trance. "Yes, that's our agenda. Skip ahead maybe 500,000 *years.*

Jimmy poked around on the keyboard. He concluded his entry and waited. Nothing happened. A shiver shot down his spine, signifying that his worst fears may be playing ***out.***

He calmly repeated the programming. When nothing happened again, he leaned forward and lowered his eyebrows. "It's not responding." He glared at Tom and Soto as he broke the news. "I'm going to gain some altitude and try a***gain.***

A somber mood prevailed, as the big jet effortlessly shot up, and continued for some time. At length, Jimmy slowed and leveled off the aircr***aft.***

Meticulously, he programmed the advance of 500,000 years, with no response to his entry. He sighed and tried again, this time shortening the time to only five years. After a few seconds, he shook his head. "We're going to have to land to trouble shoot ***this.***"

Tom and Soto bore chagrinned expressions, but offered no object***ions.***

47

CHAPTER

Jimmy sped up to search for a suitable landing site. At this high elevation, he commanded a remarkable view of the land*scape.*

The jungle was beginning to give way to hills. Soon the hills turned into rocky le*dges.*

"It's starting to look good." Tom spoke, glancing confidently at J*immy.*

Jimmy descended slightly. "I'm searching for an area that might have caves, or some kind of natural protec*tion."*

Something ahead caught his eye, and he zoomed down to investigate. "Wow, this looks promising." He half mumbled to himself. Circling around, he saw a flat area surrounded by tall rock w*alls.*

"Looks well protected." Tom sounded upbeat. The plane slowed to a hover, and gradually desce*nded.*

"Have your guns ready." Jimmy was not convinced. "We don't know if it's safe or *not."*

As the aircraft settled on the rock, each man reached for his *gun.*

Jimmy powered down the engine, which ushered in an eerie sil*ence.*

"You guys watch carefully for danger while I trouble shoot." Jimmy eyed Tom and Soto while getting up and heading for the time travel circu*itry.*

Clutching their rifles, the designated guardsmen opened the the stairway ladder, which automatically extended to the gr*ound.*

Tom cautiously looked around after his initial step to the ground. As Soto joined him, he led the way on a patrol around the jet. The rock walls rose to about 20 feet above them. As they circled around the front of the plane, Soto suddenly stopped and nudged Tom's shou**lder.**

"Look!" He pointed straight ahead. Nestled at the base of the wall were three large eggs. Tom stood speechless, but Soto slowly backed away. "This area is not safe. Eggs that big mean large dinosaurs ne**arby."**

Tom started to move back to the ladder. "We should find another spot. Let**'s go."**

As he began to climb, he was halted by a deafening roar. Blood running cold, the two men looked over their shoulders. There at the top of the cliff, was a giant carnivore. It then stepped off the ledge and landed on the flat rock, causing the ground to tre**mble.**

Snapping back to reality, Tom scampered up the ladder. Soto followed so close that he nearly climbed up Tom's **back.**

The enraged and protective beast noticed this movement, and came in like a lightning bolt. Soto felt the breeze of snapping jaws as he jumped the last three rungs, and sprawled onto the floor. A violent collision jarred the aircraft, followed by roaring and more colli**sions.**

Jimmy was just rising from the floor where he had been doing repair work. Realizing what was happening, he jumped to the pilot's chair, and utilized the cameras that gave him 160 degree vision around the plane. He quickly caught sight of the dinosaur on the plane's right side, still banging up against the **hull.**

Without hesitation, he brought the swivel gin around that was fastened to the bottom of the wing. The monster started moving to the front of the jet, but Jimmy caught him in his sights for a split second. He fired a sustained shot, which caught the creature advancing to point blank r**ange.**

Instantly the attacker fell motionless to the ground. All was si**lent.**

$$48$$

CHAPTER

"Let's get out of here!" Jimmy broadcast as he started the engine. "We don't know how many more of them there *are.*"

A sudden crash came from outside, startling everyone. "It's another one!" Tom sounded fra***ntic.***

Jimmy instantly checked the cameras. He was shocked to see that this one was twice the size of the first. Making a split second decision, he opted against attempting a take- off. His right hand turned the swivel gun until the great predator was in the cross h***airs.***

With his left hand he fired the weapon. A laser blasted the behemoth for several seconds before any effect was noticed. It stopped its advance, and tottered, as if trying to catch its balance. An ear-splitting roar was next, as the great beast fell like a tree. The crash caused the plane to jump, even on solid ***rock.***

Jimmy quickly lifted off as fast as the jet would elevate straight up. No one felt comfortable until they were out of the reach of any creature from the gr***ound.***

After reaching 200 feet, he retried going forward in time, but increased it to one million years. To his delight, he felt it working. As the disturbance came to an end, the time bubble popped. He could see the years lurch forward on the sc***reen.***

Everyone looked outside, and all were surprised that the scenery looked the ***same.***

Tom snorted in disbelief. "Are you sure we've gone for***ward?***"

Jimmy nodded. "Yes, but it certainly doesn't look lik***e it.***"

He took off, gaining altitude for a few seconds, then leveling off. "Look for wildlife." He remarked over his shoulder. "Do you see any dinos*aurs?*"

Soto searched the ground below intensely. Soon he noticed movement. "There!" He excitedly exclaimed. "Just belo*w us!*"

Jimmy flew down to get a closer look. Soon it became clear. This was a herd of duckbills running along the p*lain.*

Jimmy hovered low to get a better view, and as the three men watched, something happened. Two large predators lurched in from somewhere, honing in on one of the duckbills. The ambush was over in an instant, and the rest of the herd move*d on.*

Tom shook his head. "Our question has been answered. Glancing at Jimmy, he continued. "I think we should go forward another ten million y*ears."*

Jimmy showed no outward sign, but inside he just wanted to pack it up and go home. He had accepted this assignment, and the benefits were going to outweigh the disadvant*ages.*

"Here we go." He remarked, while typing in information. The machinery worked instantly, and soon they boomed into a vastly different w*orld.*

$$49$$

CHAPTER

Jimmy blinked twice. Looking in all directions, he saw nothing but water. No sign of land or life anyw*here.*

After a period of silence, Tom spoke up. "That's it! We've found what killed the dinosaurs. It was a catastrophic f*lood!"*

Jimmy smiled. "That does seem pretty obvious. Let's advance another 500 y*ears."*

As 500 years burst upon the scene, the water had disappe*ared.*

Nothing but hills and valleys covered the hor*izon.*

Jimmy impulsively pushed it to 5,000 years, which revealed thick green forests, but no sign of human *life.*

Like a kid with a toy, he went ahead 5 million years. People dressed in animal skins were all over, and here and there were what looked like Indian tee*pees.*

Tom stood half way up to get a better view. "This is amazing. How many years are we from our own *time?"*

Jimmy's eyebrows raised. "We're 50 million years before our *time."*

"Okay." Tom sat back down. "Let's keep going at 5 million year increments, and see what changes take p*lace."*

Taking a deep breath, Jimmy flew ahead another 5 million years. The view outside the window was dense jungle, with no sign of hu*mans.*

Tom stroked his thick mustache, but didn't speak. Jimmy took the initiative, sending the aircraft low to glide over the treetops. The view was good, but still revealed no sign of *life.*

The power was suddenly cut off, causing a lurch. Everyone looked around, panicking. Jimmy hastily fumbled around with the controls, but the plane began to drop. Down they went like a skipping rock. The underside scraped the tree tops, followed by cracking sounds and a *crash.*

All was quiet. Jimmy found himself face down on the floor. He slowly moved one arm, then the other. One leg, then the other. Nothing seemed broken. He rolled over onto his back and squi*nted.*

Tom lay not far away, moving around a little bit. A moaning sound came from his direction. "Jimmy. You alr*ight?"*

"I think so." Jimmy raised up on his hands, looking around. He saw Soto slowly pulling himself up to sit in a chair. Jimmy followed suit, gingerly grabbing a *seat.*

As Tom sat down, the three men rubbed their aches and pains for a while. Finally, Jimmy spoke up. "Look, I don't know what happened, but we're going to have to find out and fi*x it."*

Tom gazed out the window at dense jungle. "In the meantime, we have to survive." He got up and walked to the back of the cockpit. Taking three rifles from the rack, he delivered one to Jimmy, and one to Soto. "Let's see what's out t*here."*

50

CHAPTER

The three men climbed single file down the ladder, led by Jimmy. Once down on the ground, they could hear the sounds of the jungle. Automatically they all tightened their trigger *grips.*

"Let's do a little scouting." Jimmy spoke while taking a first step forward. His friends followed, but after a few feet, stopped *cold.*

A muffled growl emanated from the forest ahead. The three rifles honed in on the sound. Jimmy stood his ground, but did not advance. All was silent until he took one more step. Then came a fierce roar. The three jumped back, as tree branches snapped a*head.*

From 30 feet came a dragon-like beast at full speed. The men had time only to aim and fire. The powerful solar ray weapons had an immediate effect on the creature, which was dropped to the ground, skidding to a halt. It lay silent and motionless, just in front of *them.*

Jimmy lowered his weapon and stepped closer. The dragon's height had appeared to be 15 feet, and its length close to 25 *feet.*

Tom stood petrified, and pale. Jimmy moved around the animal, shaking his head. "I thought we were past the dino*saurs."*

Soto stepped forward, waving his rifle at the carcass. "We should travel ahead until dinosaurs are gone." Fear shown from his face. "This one could wreck your ship." Jimmy knew he was hearing wisdom from this young ancient man. He nodded, pointed toward the plane, and began wal*king.*

As they approached the plane, more aggressive sounding animals were heard. They quickened their pace, checking over their shoulders. The snapping branches and muffled roars grew louder as they scurried up the ladder and into the coc*kpit.*

Peering out the window, Jimmy was startled at what he saw. "Wow! That's a T-rex!" He quickly ran for the swivel canon controls. "Brace yourselves! He's heading this *way!"*

The T-rex appeared in the crosshairs, but before Jimmy could shoot, he rammed into the fuselage. Everyone fell flat onto the *floor.*

Hastily getting to his feet, Jimmy grabbed the swivel gun controls, and searched for a target. The carnivore's face appeared. Without warning, its mouth opened wide, and a bellowing roar burst out. The beast stepped back, looking like it was going to ram the aircraft a*gain.*

Jimmy pushed the fire button, and let him have it. A series of heavy laser shots pierced the dinosaur's chest. It back-peddled, went to its haunches, and then fell over side*ways.*

Tom's hands were visibly shaking as he flopped into a chair. Jimmy faced him and Soto, bearing a chagrinned look. "We have to get out of *here."*

<h1 style="text-align:center">51</h1>

C H A P T E R

Jimmy's legs could be seen sticking out from under the time travel panel. After a lengthy period, he scooted out and stood up. He poked a few buttons, receiving no response for his eff*orts.*

"Well, we can't travel time from the ground, but I think we can if we can get this into the air." Tom's look told of disappointment. "You know that we'll need to go outside to work one the en*gine.*"

Jimmy pursed his lips. "We'll do what we must. Here's the plan. Two of us will carry our rifles outside. One of us will stay here and man the swivel gun. He'll have to keep a sharp eye out for da*nger.*"

Tom stood and gripped his rifle as though he were leaving. "You and I will be working on the engine. He glanced at Soto. "You know how to operate the swivel gin." Soto nodded. "I have practiced a lot with this *gun.*"

Jimmy placed a hand on Soto's shoulder. "Don't hesitate to fire on anything that gets too c*lose.*"

Soto nodded. "You can trust me." Jimmy and Tom moved toward the door, while Soto peered into the scope, looking through the cross h*airs.*

Jimmy and Tom glided down the ladder, bent on a mission. They trotted to the front of the fuselage, where Jimmy held up a wrench, and snapped open a large engine *door.*

Checking all around him, Jimmy climbed a fold-out ladder, and began studying the en*gine.*

Having been drilled on all the trouble-shooting menus, he knew how to rule out most anyt*hing.*

Tom stood on the ground, keeping a close watch, and listening carefully. He could hear wildlife of many kinds, but none threate*ning.*

Jimmy ran every computer scan available, but could not identify a problem or solution. He stayed another 15 minutes just searching for loose wires, or anything haywire. Nothing was turnin*g **up.***

Wildlife began swarming in to claim the carcasses of the fallen predators. "That's it!" He announced nervously. "Let's get ***back.***"

As the pair closed the engine door and started jogging toward the cockpit ladder, they heard gun***fire.***

Glancing over their shoulders, they saw a fair-sized carnivore fall to the ground. It, and its mate bringing up the rear, looked like raptors. The men ran with renewed vigor to the ladder. Soto fired again, and the remaining pursuer tumbled ***over.***

Dozens of smaller scavengers were feeding on the carcasses, as they ran past them, and started up the la***dder.***

Danger was building by the second as they slithered up and into the coc***kpit.***

52

C H A P T E R

J immy went straight to the controls and attempted to start the engine. There was no p*ower.*

He gritted his teeth. "The crash must have pulled some wiring l*oose.*

I just don't know w*here.*"

Tom shrugged his shoulders. "Well, we have power everywhere except the en*gine.*"

"Yes." Jimmy replied, as he began manipulating the controls. "I'll check here f*irst.*"

He opened up the panel, and searched with Tom for some *time.*

Everything was intact. The three of them sat and stared at one ano*ther.* Puzzlement emanated from their *faces.*

Jimmy swiveled around in is chair. "You know, this loose wire could be anywhere around the surface of the en*gine.*"

As Tom and Soto looked on, he continued. "I'll have to squeeze into those narrow spaces in order to fin*d it.*"

Tom nodded in agreement, though his heart wasn't in it. "I really don't feel like going out there again, but what choice do we *have?*"

Jimmy and Tom trudged reluctantly down the ladder, and jogged to the nose of the plane. Without wasting time, Jimmy opened the engine door and climbed up to the top. He stepped into the empty space between the motor and the outer shell. Raising an arm up to his forehead, he flipped the flashlight fastened to his headgear. He then began a meticulous search for loose w*ires.*

Meanwhile, Tom did a continual search of their surroundings, keeping a tight grip on his high powered rifle. He started sensing the approach of a large creature. Frantically, he looked everywhere…up and down, through the t*rees.*

He brought the gun up to his shoulder, and held it. Squinting, he scanned all around, battling the late afternoon ***sun.***

Suddenly piercing the air, was the sound of a huge log being crushed. Tom felt his legs turn to rubber, and he tried to retreat, but fell on his bottom. While still on the ground, he heard a loud and fierce sounding ***roar.***

Getting up and spinning his wheels, he took off running for the cockpit. He fell twice before reaching the ladder, but did scurry up and into the p***lane.***

Meanwhile, Jimmy lay trapped between the engine and fuselage. He knew the dinosaur could sniff him out, even if he couldn't be ***seen.***

He quickly flipped off the light on his head gear, and tried to stay perfectly s***till.***

Massive footsteps drew closer and closer. They then stopped just before reaching the plane. Loud, heavy breathing commenced, followed by a roar that rocked the w***orld.***

"Come on, Soto!" Jimmy thought. "Use that gun!" He feared the beast would crash against the aircraft, which would mean curtains for him***self.***

53

CHAPTER

He felt hot air blowing into the crack. The beast became agitated, growling, and making all manner of noises. It stomped away a few steps, then bellowed loudly. This seemed to be a precursor to an at*tack.*

Suddenly the swivel gun burst into action. Its high pitched squeal was a welcome sound to Jimmy. The dinosaur shrieked in pain, before tumbling to the ground with a massive *thud.*

Jimmy took this as a cue to make his escape. He flipped on his flashlight to maneuver his way out. Just before wiggling toward the ladder, his eye caught something straight ahead…a loose wire. He quickly inched forward and examined the wire. It had been somehow pulled from under a bolt. Without hesitating, he grabbed the wire, and secured it under the bolt. Again without delay, he scooted out, still clutching his *gun.*

Climbing down the six step ladder, he glanced all around. Quickly, he scrambled toward the cockpit. Halfway there, he was cut off by two fierce looking creatures of about 7 feet tall. They did not wait long to attack. One led the way straight toward *him.*

Jimmy swiftly raised his gun and fired. The raptor-like creature fell to one side, flopping on the ground. The second one screamed loudly, exposing its sharp teeth. It bolted toward Jimmy so fast that its shot hit only the animal's leg. The beast then hit Jimmy, knocking him down and running him over. He lay flat on his back, the gun still in his right hand. At once, he rolled over onto his stomach, in time to see the predator do an about face. It didn't seem to be injured much, and seeing Jimmy, it sprinted toward *him.*

Jimmy spoke out loud to himself. "Don't miss!" He aimed carefully, and pulled the trigger. The laser hit the dinosaur's mid section, throwing it forward as it fell. Its speed was so great that it nearly fell on top of Jimmy. He stood up instantly, his arms and legs trembling uncontrollably. He started for the ladder, but his legs were like rubber, and he ended up crawling to it. He pulled himself up , mostly with his arms. Shear determination got him up and into the coc*kpit.*

His arms and knees burned like fire, as he fell to the cockpit *floor.*

Tom and Soto were there and attempted to lend a *hand.*

"Are you hurt?" A concerned Tom questioned. He bent over and reached for Jimmy. Rising to his elbows, and then his hands, he sat, leaning against a wall. He closed his eyes and panted for a while. "I fixed a loose wire. Let's see if it w*orks."*

<h1 style="text-align:center">54</h1>

<h2 style="text-align:center">C H A P T E R</h2>

Soto and Tom eagerly looked on while Jimmy sat in the pilot's chair, testing a tak*eoff.*

With one significant push of a button, the engine roared. They whooped and hollered, but Jimmy quickly focused on flying. The engine delivered full power, as the jet rose straight up at a rapid *clip.*

Peering out the window, they beheld an astonishing sight. A land teaming with dinosaurs of all kinds and s*izes.*

"This is dinosaur mecca." Tom sounded shocked, as he flopped into a c*hair.*

At a high altitude, Jimmy leveled off, and just hovered. "I'm afraid our time sequencing has been malfunctioning." He turned and eyed his two passengers. "I'm going to program this to return home, but don't expect to get t*here.*"

Tom and Soto frowned and shook their h*eads.*

The info was programmed and quickly implemented. A quivering motion commenced, followed by a hazy appearance out the window. In a few seconds, a faint boom was h*eard.*

Peering out the window, they noticed a drastic change in the vegetation. Instead of vast jungle, there was a dense evergreen forest. No large animals were in s*ight.*

Jimmy kept a lookout for a clearing. I've got to fix the time travel frequen*cies.*"

They all searched, but at the forefront of each mind was what kind of animal life was down there. "Over there!" Soto pointed to the right. There was a meadow with a fairly large clea*ring.*

Jimmy maneuvered down toward the area, decreasing speed for a better view of the surround*ings.*

As they descended slowly, nothing but trees could be seen. They were reassured by this, and unafraid to float closer to the ground, and finally touch *down.*

Jimmy kept the engine running for a moment, just as precaution. He then shut it down, and scanned the surrounding tree line for anything unu*sual.*

He looked at Tom and Soto. "I have no idea of this time period. We're just here to repair that, and then we can go *home."*

Tom nodded. "Well, while you're working on it, we'll keep a close watch out*side."*

"Okay, sounds good." Jimmy did a double take, as he grabbed his tool bag. "Careful, we don't know what's out there." He then disappeared, scooting under the instrument p*anel.*

Tom nudged Soto. "Okay, let's go." The two men opened the exit hatch and climbed down the la*dder.*

Once on the ground, Tom stood, feeling the warm breeze. Something about the atmosphere perplexed him. He couldn't put a finger o*n it.*

Flipping the gun strap from his shoulder, he looked at Soto. "Does this feel anything like your own time pe*riod?"*

Soto shook his head. He pointed to the sky. "The clouds are diffe*rent.* The sky is pink. The air is much easier to br*eath."*

Tom's eyebrows raised. "You know, that's true. Breathing is effortless, and there's just something odd about this p*lace."*

55

CHAPTER

Tom and Soto slowly started walking, keeping an eye on the tree line about 50 feet away. They reached the nose of the aircraft, then continued the circle to the other side. As they approached the halfway point, Soto stopped, and held his arm out in front of **Tom.**

"Did you hear that?" He enquired, scrutinizing the t**rees.**

Tom listened carefully for a moment. Definite noise came from somewhere in the forest. "That sounds like a mixture of gorilla and elep**hant."**

Soto was not familiar with these animals, but still became fearful. He started raising his gun, but Tom stopped him. "Don't shoot until we know if they are dange**rous."**

Branches moved suddenly, causing Soto and Tom to jump back. Out gushed a huge primate, maybe 8 feet tall. But its mass was incredibly l**arge.**

As the men back peddled, the beast moved forward with confidence, acting una**fraid.**

When it reached a too close for comfort range, Tom yelled at Soto. "Shoot to scare it ***away!***"

The two men fired all around the primate, but nothing stopped. It barged ahead, as if on a mission of destruc**tion.**

Tom knew he was going to be flattened in a matter of seconds. Aiming at the oncoming giant, he fired. Soto had the same idea, and joined the defense. The mad primate fell forward, hitting the ground like a led bal***loon.***

At that second another came barreling out of the woods, this one was very angry, and began a show of growling with intermittent scr*eams.*

The beast had extra long arms that it kept swinging, as if trying to swat at somet*hing.*

Tom and Soto looked at one another in disbelief. Tom nodded. "Shoot to kill if it comes a*t us.*"

The second primate continued its mad flurry straight toward the men. They gave it time to slow down or stop, but it sped straight at them. When it came too close, they aimed and fired, at once retreating back to the plane before any other appe*ared.*

As Tom reached the ladder, he turned and looked. His eyes popped out at the sight. Hundreds of primates poured from the forest, running toward the aircraft. "Let's go!" He shouted, and zipped like lightening up the ladder. They both literally tumbled into the cockpit, and pushed the button to raise the ladder, sealing the *door.*

"Jimmy! There's an army of them!" Tom yelled as he flew toward the swivel *gun.*

Jimmy slid out from under the instrument panel. A look of bewilderment covered his face. "What are you talking about?" He stood and looked out the wi*ndow.*

"These are huge!" Soto began explaining to him. Jimmy saw a herd of barrel chested, bigfoot-like creatures surrounding the airc*raft.*

"Okay." He shouted, as he jumped into the pilot's seat. "We're leaving *now.*"

Tom scanned around the plane with the swivel eye piece. The mass of primates started trying to tip the fuselage over. A strong rocking motion commenced as Jimmy powered up the en*gine.*

Tom did not want to fire on the group, so he held back momentarily. The rocking became severe, but up went the jet, floating toward the *sky.*

Everyone breathed a sigh of relief while they zipped straight up and out of the reach of the attacking h*orde.*

56

CHAPTER

After gaining a high altitude, Jimmy flipped into a slow cruse. He whirled his chair around to face the others. "Look." He began wagging his head. "We have no way of knowing which periods of history we've been visiting. We're literally lost in *time.*"

Tom and Soto glanced at each other. Tom covered his mustache and mouth with one hand, deep in thought. He then replied. "I know you haven't had much time to work on that, so I'm assuming that we'll keep searching for a safe place in time to get it *done.*"

"That's all we can do." Jimmy sounded exasperated. "But I don't even know if we're going backward or forward. I'll keep trying for forward, but something is broken, and I need time to fi*x it.*"

He turned and punched in some time travel data. Momentarily, and new view greeted *them.*

To Jimmy's dismay, a tall brontosaurus stood below. As they lost altitude, a great carnivore came into view, stalking the herbi*vore.*

"Look!" Soto's voice revealed excitement. "There's going to be a f*ight!*"

Jimmy hovered at a safe distance. The carnivore, who was almost as big as the brontosaurus, made some aggressive m*oves.*

The tall tree grazer backed away, showing a defensive st*ance.*

The meat eater became even more violent, rushing it, and attempting to fasten its jaws on the *neck.*

The herbivore quickly turned around, and flipped its huge tail at the attacker. It caught him on the upper body, sending him flying towards some sharp rocks. The beast landed hard, and just lay limp over the *rocks.*

"Wow!" Soto exclaimed. "That was ama*zing!*"

"I take it this won't be a prime spot to land." Tom a*dded.*

Jimmy frowned. "No. It's like we're stuck in prehistoric time. There must be a period before or after dinosaurs that's *safe.*"

"Maybe," Tom looked up, "since it's broken, we're pretty much staying in the same pe*riod.*"

Jimmy shook his head. "The primates were not in dinosaur times. It's just throwing us all over the *map.*"

"Well," Tom advised, "just keep trying until we get what we *want.*"

Jimmy bit his lower lip in frustration. He busied himself at the controls, programming a jump to as far into the future as poss*ible.*

Momentarily, the world outside the cockpit changed. As the three men looked at the scene, they saw no trees…just rolling hills. There was no animal life notice*able.*

"Good!" Jimmy's voice rang with excitement. "We are going to land here and get this thing repa*ired.*"

Drifting low, and finally touching ground, he powered down. All was totally si*lent.*

Jimmy grabbed his tools and once again wasted no time, swiftly scooting under the instrument p*anel.*

Tom and Soto peered out the window, and saw nothing but wild *grass.*

57

CHAPTER

After the events of the last few stops, they opted to stay in the coc***kpit.***

Jimmy worked feverishly to trouble shoot the system. An hour went by, and he was still running t***ests.***

Tom and Soto spotted no animal life so far. Tom began to fear the possibility that they were in the aftermath of nuclear war***fare.***

Another hour passed, and Jimmy crawled out from the access hole. He stood at the control panel pushing buttons, and pecking at the keyb***oard.***

Suddenly he stopped and stared. "What?" He uttered loudly in disbelief. Tom and Soto quickly got up and stepped to the computer screen. "Is it working now?" Tom wondered anxio***usly.***

Jimmy looked at his travel mates. "This is 500 million BC." Just saying it stunned him, causing him to shake his ***head.***

Tom and Soto had no response. They just stared at the sc***reen.***

Jimmy went on. "It should work properly now. We'll take off and give it a ***shot."***

A few minutes later they were soaring high in the sky. He once again hovered the aircraft, after which he stood there rubbing his hands toge***ther.***

"Alright, gentlemen." He turned and entered coordinates into the computer. "We are going back to your time, ***Tom."***

All was silent as the time travel cycle finished. They then peered out the wi***ndow.***

A great whoop & holler went up because the landscape revealed the tall skyscrapers of ***2280.***

"We're home!" Tom shouted, thrusting a fist into the air. Jimmy flashed a grin as he steered the aircraft in for a landing. "I hope your curiosity is satis*fied.*"

Tom chuckled and nodded. "Yes. At least for *now.*"

Within a few minutes the plane had landed at the airfield. The men just sat there, saying nothing for a w*hile.*

"Well, that was a trip for the ages." Tom remarked. "Let's meet tomorrow morning to discuss where we go from *here.*"

Upon disembarking the plane, not a soul was there to meet them. This was fine with Jimmy, who felt exhausted. He just wanted to be left alone to collect his thoughts and get a good night's *sleep.*

Finally stepping into his apartment, he walked over to the couch and sort of fell ont*o it.*

58

Chapter

Ten hours later, Jimmy was awakened by a call from Tom. The meeting was to be at his of*fice.*

Jimmy had time to clean up and grab some breakfast before heading out the door. When he arrived, Soto was already t*here.*

Tom seemed chipper and full of life, extending his arm toward a table and chairs. "Have a seat, Jimmy. We've got some things to go *over.*"

When all were seated, Tom stroked his over-sized moustache. A smile was still evident, as he took a deep breath and exhaled. "This eventful trip we just took was historical. What I mean by that is we are going to hold a patent on the time mac*hine.*"

He looked at Jimmy. "And you, my friend, will get credit for its invention." He held up his hand. "Now I know that you worked with other scientists, but that was in your own time. You have now reinvented it." He glanced at Soto. "You are part of this team, and will remai*n so.*"

He leaned back in his chair and smiled. "Gentlemen, we are going to be rich and famous. Get used t*o it.*"

Jimmy raised his eyebrows, and nervously caressed his chin. He pursed his lips and nodded. "Sounds good." He began with an understatement. "So what's the plan from *here?*"

Tom made a sweeping gesture. "For starters, we'll set up contacts with journalists and authors. We'll also arrange paid trips for whoever has the m*oney.*"

After a brief silence, Tom looked from Jimmy to Soto. "Oh, don't worry. You'll have plenty of time to do whatever else you want. We'll be flex*ible.*"

Jimmy folded his hands and looked briefly up at the ceiling. "Very good. When I get the time, I'm going to visit the 21st century. I have a little something planned for a certain j*udge.*"

59

Chapter

A southern California judge was walking between buildings on his usual lunch break. He'd had a typical morning of three convictions. Two of them would be sent to the Cretaceous pe*riod.*

He smugly straightened his necktie, while glaring at passe*rsby.*

As the sidewalk broke into a clearing, he felt a sudden breeze, accompanied by a shimmering sensation. He looked around, trying to determine what was happe*ning.*

He was suddenly closed in and couldn't move. His entire body became weightless, and began to fly through the air. The judge was sure he was being abducted by al*iens.*

Jimmy worked studiously at a section of the control panel labelled 'Circumference Trans*port'.*

"It's working nicely!" He announced. Tom and Soto stood next to him watching with great int*erest.*

"The tractor beam has pulled him right up by the fuselage." Jimmy clenched his fist and thrust his arm, in a triumphant ges*ture.*

"Okay, here we go to the Cretaceous pe*riod."*

Tom and Soto said nothing, just observing the whole t*hing.*

Soon the scene outside changed to prehistoric tropics. Below could be seen all manner of wildlife, including dinos*aurs.*

Jimmy lowered his altitude, coming very close to the ground. He released the judge on the ground, and ascended a short distance into the *sky.*

The judge was frantic. He knew where he was, and now assumed that he was being punished for all the prisoners he had sent **here.**

He stood there looking one way, then another, not sure where to go or what t**o do.**

From Jimmy's position, he could see several dangerous animals close by. One was travelling in the judge's direction. He continued hovering, and simply wa**ited.**

Meanwhile the judge was sweating it out. He could hear wild beasts all around him, including ferocious roars of the huge carniv**ores.**

Then it happened. He saw a great predator approaching him. Quickly he began backtracking, and broke into a dead run. The hunter spotted him, and started sprinting toward **him.**

The judge yelled and hollered as he ran, looking up at the plane above him, pleading for **help.**

Jimmy knew it would only be a few seconds to the judge's doom unless he intervened. He deployed the circumference transport tractor beam, and pull up o**n it.**

The judge rose rapidly into the air, but still narrowly missed a set of snapping **jaws.**

At a safe distance, Jimmy hovered, immediately engaging time travel to the 21st cen**tury.**

CHAPTER

60

The aircraft came down close to the judge's drop-off point. While hovering, he walked over to the trap door. Reaching to the floor, he grasped the handle and pulled open the **door.**

Peering up at him was the judge…his body suspended by the circumference transport **beam.**

Jimmy's face bore a stern look as he spoke. "No one deserves to be sent there. I don't care what their crime is." He started to close the door, but held up. "By the way, I didn't do it. My name is Jimmy Br**ooks."**

He slammed the door over the judge's head. Coldly, he stood up and walked over to the pilot's c**hair.**

The hovering jet quickly descended to the ground. Suddenly the judge was released, falling two feet and rolling over the **lawn.**

Getting to his feet, he looked up in time to see the jet zoom off. He stood there shaking his head, thinking about what just happened. Turning around slowly, he started mulling over his sentencing pract**ices.**

Meanwhile, Jimmy had gone forward to the 23rd century, and was heading home. A smile broke out over Tom's face as he stood facing Jimmy and Soto. "Well, I can promise you both plenty of excitement if you'll stay on." Shifting his feet, he continued. "You know the money's great. We'll be doing a whole lot more experimentation with time tr**avel."**

Jimmy swiveled around in his chair, pushed a couple buttons on the control panel, then stood. "I think I can speak for Soto. We'd love to do this." He glanced at Soto before continuing. "You couldn't get a better gig anyw**here."**

"Of course, Tom added, "you'll both have to deal with the media. We are all famous now, so learn to deal wit*h it.*"

Soto laughed. "This is all new to me, but it's fun. If I can, I want to learn to fly this p*lane.*"

"That can be arranged." Tom reassured him. "But why don't we take two weeks off to recuperate. We could all us*e it.*"

He held up one hand. "The rediscovery of time travel is a great historical milestone. And Soto, you made the adjustment from a primitive, prehistoric society. That's quite a *feat.*"

He shook both their hands, and grinned proudly. "Congratulations, gentl*emen!*"